'What matters is to live everything. *Live* the questions for now.'

U0874664

RAINER MARIA RILKE

Letters to a Young Poet

Translated by
Charlie Louth

Preface

In late autumn 1902 it was – I was sitting under ancient chestnut trees in the gardens of the Military Academy in Wiener Neustadt with a book. I was so absorbed by my reading that I hardly noticed it when the only one of our teachers who was not an army officer, Horaček, the learned and good-natured chaplain of the Academy, came and joined me. He took the volume from my hand, looked at the cover and shook his head. 'Poems by Rainer Maria Rilke?' he asked thoughtfully. He leafed through its pages, ran his eyes over a few verses, looked reflectively into the distance and finally nodded. 'So, our pupil René Rilke has become a poet.'

And I was told about the slight, pale boy sent by his parents more than fifteen years before to the Military Lower School in Sankt Pölten so that he might later become an officer. In those days Horaček had worked there as the chaplain and he still remembered his former pupil well. He described him as a quiet, serious, highly gifted child, who liked to keep himself to himself, put up with the discipline of boarding-school life patiently and after the fourth year moved on with the others to the Military Upper School in Mährisch-Weisskirchen. There his constitution proved not to be resilient enough, and so his parents took him out of the establishment and had him continue his studies at home in Prague. What path his career had taken after that Horaček was unable to say.

Given all this it is probably not difficult to understand that I decided that very hour to send my poetic efforts to Rainer Maria Rilke and ask him for his verdict. Not yet twenty years old and on the verge of going into a profession which I felt was directly opposed to my true inclinations, I thought that if anyone was going to understand my situation it was the author of the book To Celebrate Myself. *And without its being my express intention, my verses were accompanied by a letter in which I revealed myself more unreservedly than to anyone ever before, or to anyone since.*

Many weeks went by before an answer came. The letter with its blue seal bore a Paris postmark, weighed heavy in the hand and displayed on the envelope the same clarity, beauty and assurance of hand with which the content itself was written from the first line to the last. And so my regular correspondence with Rainer Maria Rilke began, lasting until 1908 and then gradually petering out because life forced me into domains which the poet's warm, tender and moving concern had precisely wanted to protect me from.

But that is unimportant. The only important thing is the ten letters that follow, important for the insight they give into the world in which Rainer Maria Rilke lived and worked, and important too for many people engaged in growth and change, today and in the future. And where a great and unique person speaks, the rest of us should be silent.

Franz Xaver Kappus
Berlin, June 1929

Paris, 17 February 1903

Dear Sir,

Your letter only reached me a few days ago. Let me thank you for the great and endearing trust it shows. There is little more I can do. I cannot go into the nature of your verses, for any critical intention is too remote from me. There is nothing less apt to touch a work of art than critical words: all we end up with there is more or less felicitous misunderstandings. Things are not all as graspable and sayable as on the whole we are led to believe; most events are unsayable, occur in a space that no word has ever penetrated, and most unsayable of all are works of art, mysterious existences whose life endures alongside ours, which passes away.

Having begun with this preliminary remark, all I will go on to say is that your verses have no identity of their own, though they do have tacit and concealed hints of something personal. I feel that most clearly in the last poem, 'My Soul'. There something individual is trying to come into words, to find its manner. And in the lovely poem 'To Leopardi' perhaps a kind of affinity with this great and solitary man develops. Still, the poems are not yet anything in themselves, nothing self-sufficient, not even the last one and the one to Leopardi. The kind letter you wrote accompanying them does not fail to make many of the shortcomings I sensed in reading your verses explicable, without for all that being able to give them a name.

You ask whether your verses are good. You ask me that. You have asked others, before. You send them to magazines. You compare them with other poems, and you worry when certain editors turn your efforts down. Now (since you have allowed me to offer you advice) let me ask you to give up all that. You are looking to the outside, and that above all you should not be doing now. Nobody can advise you and help you, nobody. There is only one way. Go into yourself. Examine the reason that bids you to write; check whether it reaches its roots into the deepest region of your heart, admit to yourself whether you would die if it should be denied you to write. This above all: ask yourself in your night's quietest hour: *must* I write? Dig down into yourself for a deep answer. And if it should be affirmative, if it is given to you to respond to this serious question with a loud and simple '*I must*', then construct your life according to this necessity; your life right into its most inconsequential and slightest hour must become a sign and witness of this urge. Then approach nature. Then try, like the first human being, to say what you see and experience and love and lose. Don't write love poems; avoid at first those forms which are too familiar and habitual: they are the hardest, for you need great maturity and strength to produce something of your own in a domain where good and sometimes brilliant examples have been handed down to us in abundance. For this reason, flee general subjects and take refuge in those offered by your own day-to-day life; depict your sadnesses and desires, passing thoughts and faith in some kind of beauty – depict all this with intense, quiet, humble sincerity and make use of whatever you find about you to express yourself, the images from your dreams and the things in your memory. If your everyday life seems to lack material, do not blame it; blame yourself, tell yourself that you are not poet enough to summon up its riches, for there is no lack for him who creates and no poor, trivial place. And even if you were in a prison whose walls did not let any of the sounds of the world outside reach your senses – would you not have your childhood still, this marvellous, lavish source, this treasure-house of memories? Turn your attention towards that. Attempt to raise the sunken sensations of this distant past; your self will become the stronger for it, your loneliness will open up and become a twilit dwelling in which the noise other people make is only heard far off. And if from this turn inwards, from this submersion in your own world, there come *verses*, then it will not occur to you to ask anyone whether they are good verses. Nor will you attempt to interest magazines in these bits of work: for in them you will see your beloved natural possessions, a piece, and a voice, of your life. A work of art is good if it has arisen out of necessity. The verdict on it lies in this nature of its origin: there is no other. For this reason, my dear Sir, the only advice I have is this: to go into yourself and to examine the depths from which your life springs; at its source you will find the answer to the question of whether you *have* to write. Accept this answer as it is, without seeking to interpret it. Perhaps it will turn out that you are called to be an artist. Then assume this fate and bear it, its burden and its greatness, without ever asking after the rewards that may come from outside. For he who creates must be a world of his own and find everything within himself and in the natural world that he has elected to follow.

But perhaps even after this descent into yourself and into your solitariness you will have to give up the idea of becoming a poet (the feeling that one could live without writing is enough, as I said, to make it something one should never do). But even then, to have taken pause in the way I am asking you to will not have been in vain. Whatever happens, your life will find its own paths from that point on, and that they may be good, productive and far-reaching is something I wish for you more than I can say.

What else should I say to you? I think everything has been emphasized as it should be; and all I wanted to do in the end was advise you to go through your development quietly and seriously; you cannot disrupt it more than by looking outwards and expecting answers from without to questions that only your innermost instinct in your quietest moments will perhaps be able to answer.

I was delighted to find Professor Horaček's name in your letter; I retain a great admiration for this kind-hearted scholar, a gratitude that has endured over the years. Could you please pass on these sentiments to him; it is very kind of him still to remember me, and I much appreciate it.

The verses you were so good as to entrust me with I am sending back to you along with this letter. Thank you again for the extent and the warmth of your trust – as well as I can, I have attempted with this sincere reply to make myself a little worthier of it than, as a stranger, I really am.

With all devotion and sympathy,

Rainer Maria Rilke

Viareggio near Pisa (Italy), 5 April 1903

You must forgive me, my dear Sir, for only attending to your letter of 24 February today: the whole time I have been under the weather, not ill exactly but oppressed by an influenza-like feebleness which has made me incapable of anything. And in the end, when all else had failed, I travelled down to this southern coast, whose beneficial effects have helped me in the past. But I'm still not well again, writing is difficult, and so you must take these few lines as if there were more of them.

First of all you should know that every letter from you will always be a pleasure, and you only need to be understanding with regard to the replies, which often, maybe, will leave you with empty hands; for at bottom, and particularly in the deepest and most important things, we are unutterably alone, and for one person to be able to advise, let alone help, another, a great deal must come about, a great deal must come right, a whole constellation of things must concur for it to be possible at all.

There are just two things I wanted to say to you today:

Irony: don't let yourself be ruled by it, especially not in uncreative moments. In creative ones try to make use of it as one means among many to get a grasp on life. Used purely, it too is pure, and there is no need to be ashamed of it; and if you feel too familiar with it, if you fear your intimacy is growing too much, then turn towards great and serious subjects, next to which irony becomes small and helpless. Seek out the depths of things: irony will never reach down there – and if in so doing you come up against something truly great, inquire whether this way of relating to things originates in a necessary part of your being. For under the influence of serious things irony will either fall away (if it is something incidental) or on the contrary (if it really belongs to you in a native way) it will gain strength and so become a serious tool and take its place among the means with which you will be bound to create your art.

And the second thing I wanted to tell you today is this:

Of all my books there are only a few I cannot do without, and two are always among my effects, wherever I am. I have them with me here: the Bible, and the books of the great Danish writer *Jens Peter Jacobsen*. I wonder whether you know his works. They are easy to get hold of, because a number of them are available in good translations in Reclam's Universal-Bibliothek. Get hold of the little volume *Six Novellas* by J. P. Jacobsen, and his novel *Niels Lyhne*, and begin with the first story in the first of these volumes which is called 'Mogens'. A world will come over you, the joy, the richness, the incomprehensible greatness of a new world. Live in these books for a while, learn from them what seems to be worth learning, but above all love them. This love will be repaid you thousands and thousands of times, and however your life may turn out – this love, I am sure of it, will run through the weave of your becoming as one of the most important threads of all among the other threads of your experiences, disappointments and joys.

If I had to say from whom I have learnt anything about the nature of artistic creation, about its profundity and eternity, there are only two names I can give: *Jacobsen's*, the great, great poet, and *Auguste Rodin's*, the sculptor who has no equal among all artists now alive. –

All success on your paths!

Yours,

Rainer Maria Rilke

Viareggio near Pisa (Italy), 23 April 1903

Your Easter letter, my dear Sir, gave me a great deal of pleasure, for it had many good things to report, and the way you spoke about Jacobsen's great and generous art showed me that I was not mistaken in conducting your life and its many questions to this source of plenty.

Now *Niels Lyhne* will reveal itself to you, a book full of splendours and depths; the more often one reads it, it seems to contain everything, from life's faintest scent to the full, grand savour of its heaviest fruits. There is nothing in it that has not been understood, grasped, lived, and known in memory's trembling, lingering resonance; no experience is too slight, and the merest occurrence unfolds like a fate, and fate itself is like a wonderful, vast fabric in which every thread is drawn by an infinitely tender hand and laid next to another, held in place and supported by a hundred others. You will experience the immense pleasure of reading this book for the first time, and will pass through its innumerable surprises as if in a new dream. But I can tell you that later too one always traverses these books with the same astonishment and that they lose nothing of the wondrous power, relinquish none of the magical qualities, which they lavish on the reader the first time round.

One just takes more and more enjoyment in them, one grows ever more grateful and somehow better and simpler in seeing the world, deeper in one's faith in life and happier and larger in living. –

And later you must read the wonderful book of the fate and longings of *Marie Grubbe* and Jacobsen's letters and diaries and fragments and finally his verse which (even if the translations are only moderate) has an infinite resonance. (To do so, I'd suggest you buy the lovely collected edition of Jacobsen's works – which has all this in it – if you get the opportunity. It came out in three volumes and in good translations with Eugen Diederichs in Leipzig and costs, I believe, only 5 or 6 marks a volume.)

In your opinion on 'Here roses should stand . . .' (a work of such incomparable subtlety and form) you are of course absolutely in the right, and inviolably so, whatever the author of the preface may have to say. And let me at once make this request: read as little as possible in the way of aesthetics and criticism – it will either be partisan views, fossilized and made meaningless in its lifeless rigidity, or it will be neat wordplay, where one opinion will triumph one day and the opposite the next. Works of art are infinitely solitary and nothing is less likely to reach them than criticism. Only love can grasp them and hold them and do them justice. – With regard to any such disquisition, review or introduction, trust yourself and your instincts; even if you go wrong in your judgement, the natural growth of your inner life will gradually, over time, lead you to other insights. Allow your verdicts their own quiet untroubled development which like all progress must come from deep within and cannot be forced or accelerated. *Everything* must be carried to term before it is born. To let every impression and the germ of every feeling come to completion inside, in the dark, in the unsayable, the unconscious, in what is unattainable to one's own intellect, and to wait with deep humility and patience for the hour when a new clarity is delivered: that alone is to live as an artist, in the understanding and in one's creative work.

These things cannot be measured by time, a year has no meaning, and ten years are nothing. To be an artist means: not to calculate and count; to grow and ripen like a tree which does not hurry the flow of its sap and stands at ease in the spring gales without fearing that no summer may follow. It will come. But it comes only to those who are patient, who are simply there in their vast, quiet tranquillity, as if eternity lay before them. It is a lesson I learn every day amid hardships I am thankful for: *patience* is all!

RICHARD DEHMEL: With his books (as also, by the way, with the man himself whom I know slightly) I always find myself, when I've come upon one of his best pages, fearful of the next, which can always undo it all again and turn what was so lovely into something base. You sum him up very well with your phrase about 'living and writing in rut'. – And indeed artistic experience lies so incredibly close to sexual experience, to its pains and pleasures, that both phenomena are really just different forms of one and the same desire and felicity. And if instead of speaking of 'rut' we could say 'sex', sex in the large, capacious, pure sense, not rendered suspect by any misapprehensions stemming from the Church, his art would be very great and infinitely important. His poetic power is immense, as vigorous as instinct; it has its own reckless rhythms running through it and bursts out of him as if from a mountain.

But this power seems not always to be quite genuine and free of affectation. (But then that is one of the severest tests of an artist: he must always remain innocent and unconscious of his greatest virtues if he is to avoid depriving them of their uninhibitedness and purity.) And when this power, coursing through his being, reaches his sexuality, it doesn't find quite the pure human being it needs. The world of sexuality it finds is not entirely mature and pure, it is not *human* enough, only *virile*, rut, intoxication, restlessness, and weighed down by the old prejudices and arrogance with which men have disfigured and overburdened love. Because he loves *only* as a man, not as a human being, there is in his sense of sexuality something narrow, seemingly savage, hateful, time-bound, uneternal that diminishes his art and makes it ambivalent and doubtful. It is not without blemish, it is marked by the times and by passion, and little of it will prevail and endure. (But that's the case with most art!) In spite of all this one can still take deep pleasure in what is great about his work and must just make sure not to lose oneself to it and become an acolyte of this Dehmel-world which is so full of anxiety, of adultery and confusion, and remote from the real destinies, which create more suffering than these passing afflictions but also give more opportunity for greatness and more courage to make something that will last.

To come to my own books, really I'd like to send you all those that might give pleasure. But I am very poor, and as soon as my books have appeared they cease to belong to me. I cannot buy them myself and, as I'd so often like to, give them to those who would value and look after them.

For that reason I have written down for you on a slip of paper the titles (and publishing houses) of my recent books (that is the very newest, altogether I must have published 12 or 13) and must leave it to you, dear Sir, to order one or two of them if they take your fancy.

I shall be glad to know that my books are with you.

All good wishes,

Yours,

Rainer Maria Rilke

at present in Worpswede near Bremen, 16 July 1903

About ten days ago I left Paris, ailing and very weary, and travelled to these great northern plains whose vastness and quiet and sky are supposed to return my health to me. But I drove into unceasing rain which only today is beginning to clear a bit over the restless, windswept land; and I'm using this first moment of brightness to send you a greeting, my dear Sir.

My dear Mr Kappus: I have left your letter unanswered for a long time – not that I had forgotten it; on the contrary, it was the kind of letter one reads again, coming across it among one's papers, and I recognized you in it as if I were in your presence. It was your letter of the second of May – I'm sure you remember it. When, as I do now, I read it in the great calm of these expanses, I am touched by your fine concern for life, even more than I was in Paris where everything has a different tone and gets lost in the immense din which sets things trembling. Here, surrounded as I am by a mighty stretch of land over which the winds blow in from seas, here I feel that no human being anywhere can respond to those questions and feelings that have a profound life of their own; for even the best of us get the words wrong when we want them to express such intangible and almost unsayable things. But all the same I believe that you need not remain without solution if you hold to things like those now refreshing my eyes. If you hold close to nature, to what is simple in it, to the small things people hardly see and which all of a sudden can become great and immeasurable; if you have this love for what is slight, and quite unassumingly, as a servant, seek to win the confidence of what seems poor – then everything will grow easier, more unified and somehow more conciliatory, not perhaps in the intellect, which, amazed, remains a step behind, but in your deepest consciousness, watchfulness and knowledge. You are so young, all still lies ahead of you, and I should like to ask you, as best I can, dear Sir, to be patient towards all that is unresolved in your heart and to try to love *the questions themselves* like locked rooms, like books written in a foreign tongue. Do not now strive to uncover answers: they cannot be given you because you have not been able to live them. And what matters is to live everything. *Live* the questions for now. Perhaps then you will gradually, without noticing it, live your way into the answer, one distant day in the future. Perhaps you do carry within yourself the possibility of forming and creating, as a particularly happy and pure way of living. School yourself for it, but take what comes in complete trust, and as long as it is a product of your will, of some kind of inner necessity, accept it and do not despise it. Sex is difficult, true. But difficult things are what we were set to do, almost everything serious is difficult, and everything is serious. If you only acknowledge this and manage from your own resources, from your own disposition and nature, from your own experience and childhood and strength, to win your way towards a relationship to sex that is wholly your own (*not* influenced by convention and custom), then you have no need to fear losing yourself and becoming unworthy of your best possession.

Physical desire is a sensual experience, no different from pure contemplation or the pure sensation with which a fine fruit sates the tongue; it is a great and endless feeling which is granted to us, a way of knowing the world, the fullness and the splendour of all knowledge. And that we receive this pleasure cannot be a bad thing; what is bad is the way almost all of us misuse the experience and waste it and apply it as a stimulus to the tired parts of our lives, as a distraction instead of as a concentration of ourselves into climactic points. Eating, too, has been turned away from its true nature: want on the one hand and superfluity on the other have troubled the clarity of this need, and all the profound, simple necessities in which life renews itself have similarly been obscured. But the individual can clarify them for himself and live in this clearness (and if not the individual, who is too dependent, then at least the solitary). He can remind himself that all beauty in plants and animals is a quiet and durable form of love and longing, and he can see the animal, as also the plant, patiently and willingly joining and multiplying and growing, not from physical pleasure, not from physical suffering, but bowing to necessities which are greater than pleasure and pain and more powerful than desire and resistance. Oh if only mankind could embrace this mystery, which penetrates the earth right into its smallest elements, with more humility, and bear and sustain it with more gravity and know how terribly heavy it is, instead of taking it lightly. If only mankind could hold its own fertility in awe, which is one and the same whether it manifests itself in the spirit or in the flesh. For creativity of the spirit has its origin in the physical kind, is of one nature with it and only a more delicate, more rapt and less fleeting version of the carnal sort of sex. 'The desire to be a creator, to engender, to give form' is nothing without its continuing, palpable confirmation and realization in the world, nothing without the myriad expressions of assent coming from animals and things. And the pleasure it gives is only as unutterably fine and abundant as it is because it is full of inherited memories of the engendering and bearing of millions. In one creative thought a thousand forgotten nights of love revive and lend it grandeur and height. And those who come together in the night-time and are entwined in a cradle of desire are carrying out a serious work in collecting sweetness, profundity and strength for the song of some poet yet to come, who will rise up to speak unutterable pleasures. And they summon up the future; and even if they err and embrace one another blindly, the future will come all the same, a new creature will appear, and based on the chance act that seems to be accomplished here the law comes into being according to which a resistant and vigorous seed forces its way through to the egg moving forward to receive it. Do not be distracted by surfaces; it is in the depths that all laws obtain. And those who live the mystery falsely and badly (and there are many of them) forfeit it only for themselves and still hand it on like a sealed letter, unwittingly. And don't be put off by the multiplicity of names and the complexity of the various cases. Perhaps a great maternity lies over everything, as a shared longing. The beauty of the virgin, of a being, who, as you put it so well, 'has not yet achieved anything', is maternity divining and preparing itself, anxious and full of longing. And the beauty of a mother is maternity at work, and that of the old woman a great memory. And in the man too there is maternity, as it seems to me, physical and spiritual; his engendering is also a kind of giving birth, and it is an act of birth when he creates out of his inmost resources. And perhaps the sexes are more closely related than we think, and the great renewal of the world will perhaps consist in man and woman, freed of all sense of error and disappointment, seeking one another out not as opposites but as brothers and sisters and neighbours, and they will join together as *human beings*, to share the heavy weight of sexuality that is laid upon them with simplicity, gravity and patience.

But everything which one day will perhaps be possible for many, the solitary individual can prepare for and build now with his hands which are more unerring. For this reason, dear Mr Kappus, love your solitude and bear the pain it causes you with melody wrought with lament. For the people who are close to you, you tell me, are far away, and that shows that you are beginning to create a wider space around you. And if what is close is far, then the space around you is wide indeed and already among the stars; take pleasure in your growth, in which no one can accompany you, and be kind-hearted towards those you leave behind, and be assured and gentle with them and do not plague them with your doubts or frighten them with your confidence or your joyfulness, which they cannot understand. Look for some kind of simple and loyal way of being together with them which does not necessarily have to alter however much you may change; love in them a form of life different from your own and show understanding for the older ones who fear precisely the solitude in which you trust. Avoid providing material for the drama which always spans between parents and their children; it saps much of the children's strength and consumes that parental love which works and warms even when it does not comprehend. Ask no advice of them and reckon with no understanding; but believe in a love which is stored up for you like an inheritance, and trust that in this love there is a strength and a benediction out of whose sphere you do not need to issue even if your journey is a long one.

It is good that for the moment you are going into a profession which will make you independent and mean you only have yourself to rely on, in every sense. Have the patience to wait and see whether your inmost life feels confined by the form of this occupation. I consider it a very difficult and a very demanding one, as it is burdened by powerful conventions and leaves almost no room to interpret its duties according to your own lights. But your solitude, even in the midst of quite foreign circumstances, will be a hold and a home for you, and leading from it you will find all the paths you need. All my good wishes are ready to accompany you, and you have all my confidence and trust.

Yours,

Rainer Maria Rilke

Rome, 29 October 1903

My dear Sir,

Your letter of 29 August reached me in Florence, and only now – two months on – do I give you news of it. Forgive me this delay, but I prefer not to write letters when I'm travelling because letter-writing requires more of me than just the basic wherewithal: some quiet and time on my own and a moment when I feel relatively at home.

We arrived in Rome about six weeks ago, at a time when it was still the empty, hot city, the Rome supposedly ridden with fevers, and this circumstance, together with other practical difficulties to do with settling in, meant that the unrest surrounding us went on and on and the foreignness of the place lay on us with the weight of homelessness. On top of that you have to remember that Rome (if one is not yet acquainted with it) seems oppressively sad when one first arrives: the lifeless and drear museum-atmosphere it breathes, the abundance of fragments of the past (on which a tiny present nourishes itself) that have been fetched out of the ground and laboriously maintained, the unspeakable excess of esteem, nourished by academics and philologists with the help of run-of-the-mill tourists, given to all these disfigured and spoilt objects which after all are basically nothing more than accidental vestiges of another age and of a life that is not our own and is not meant to be. At last, after weeks of daily fending off, you get your bearings back, and somewhat dazed you tell yourself: No, there is not *more* beauty here than elsewhere, and all these objects which generation after generation have continued to admire, which inexpert hands have mended and restored, they mean nothing, are nothing and have no heart and no value; but there is a great deal of beauty here, because there is beauty everywhere. Infinitely lively waters go over the old aqueducts into the city and on the many squares dance over bowls of white stone and fill broad capacious basins and murmur all day and raise their murmur into the night, which is vast and starry and soft with winds. And there are gardens here, unforgettable avenues and flights of steps, steps conceived by Michelangelo, steps built to resemble cascades of flowing water – giving birth to step after broad step like wave after wave as they descend the incline. With the help of such impressions you regain your composure, win your way back out of the demands of the talking and chattering multitude (how voluble it is!), and you slowly learn to recognize the very few things in which something everlasting can be felt, something you can love, something solitary in which you can take part in silence.

I'm still living in the city, on the Capitol, not far from the finest equestrian statue that has come down to us from Roman art – that of Marcus Aurelius. But in a few weeks I shall be moving into a quiet, simple room, an old summer-house lost in the depths of a great park, hidden away from the city with its noise and its inconsequentiality. I'll live there for the whole winter and take pleasure in the great stillness from which I expect the gift of good and productive hours . . .

From there, where I shall feel more at home, I'll write you a longer letter in which I'll also have something to say about your writing. Today I must just mention (and it was perhaps wrong of me not to have done so before) that the book you announced in your letter (which you said contained pieces by you) has not arrived here. Has it been sent back to you, perhaps from Worpswede? (For: packets cannot be forwarded abroad.) This is the best explanation, which it would be nice to have confirmed. I hope it has not gone astray, which given the Italian postal service cannot be ruled out – alas.

I should have been glad to receive the book (as with everything that gives some sign of you); and any verse you have written since I shall always (if you entrust me with it) read and reread and take in as well and as completely as I can. With good wishes and greetings,

Yours,

Rainer Maria Rilke

Rome, 23 December 1903

My dear Mr Kappus,

You shall not go without greetings from me at Christmas time, when you are perhaps finding your solitude harder than usual to bear among all the festivities. But if you notice that it is great, then be glad of it; for what (you must ask yourself) would a solitude be that was not great? There is only *one* solitude, and it is vast and not easy to bear and almost everyone has moments when they would happily exchange it for some form of company, be it ever so banal or trivial, for the illusion of some slight correspondence with whoever one happens to come across, however unworthy . . . But perhaps those are precisely the hours when solitude grows, for its growth is painful like the growth of boys and sad like the beginning of spring. But that must not put you off. What is needed is this, and this alone: solitude, great inner loneliness. Going into oneself and not meeting anyone for hours – that is what one must arrive at. Loneliness of the kind one knew as a child, when the grown-ups went back and forth bound up in things which seemed grave and weighty because they looked so busy, and because one had no idea what they were up to.

And when one day you realize that their preoccupations are meagre, their professions barren and no longer connected to life, why not continue to look on them like a child, as if on something alien, drawing on the depths of your own world, on the expanse of your own solitude, which itself is work and achievement and a vocation? Why wish to exchange a child's wise incomprehension for rejection and contempt, when incomprehension is solitude, whereas rejection and contempt are ways of participating in what, by precisely these means, you want to sever yourself from?

Think, dear Mr Kappus, of the world that you carry within you, and call this thinking whatever you like. Whether it is memory of your own childhood or longing for your own future – just be attentive towards what rises up inside you, and place it above everything that you notice round about. What goes on in your innermost being is worth all your love, this is what you must work on however you can and not waste too much time and too much energy on clarifying your attitude to other people. Who says you have such an attitude at all? – I know, your profession is hard and goes against you, and I had foreseen your complaints and knew they would come. Now that they have come I cannot assuage them; I can only advise you to consider whether all professions are not like that, full of demands, full of hostility for the individual, steeped as it were in the hatred of those who with sullen resentment have settled for a life of sober duty. The station you are now obliged to occupy is no more heavily burdened with conventions, prejudices and misapprehensions than any other, and if there are some domains that make a show of greater freedom there are none that are vast and spacious and in contact with the great things of which real life consists. Only the solitary individual is subject, like a thing, to the fundamental laws, and if someone goes out into the morning as it is breaking, or looks out into the evening full of occurrence, and if he feels what is happening there, every hint of station slips from him as if from a dead man, although he is standing in the midst of life itself. Dear Mr Kappus, something similar to what you now have to undergo as an officer would have affected you in any of the existing professions, and even if, outside of any position, you had sought only fleeting and non-committal contact with society, you would not have been spared this feeling of constraint. – It is the same everywhere; but that is no reason for anxiety or sadness; if there is no communal feeling between you and other people, try to be near to things – they will not abandon you. The nights are still there and the winds that go through the trees and over the many lands; among things and among animals all is still full of happenings in which you can take part; and the children are still as you were when you were a child, just as sad and happy, and whenever you think of your childhood you live among them again, among the lonely children, and adults are nothing and their dignity has no worth.

And if it frightens and pains you to think of your childhood and of the simplicity and stillness that go together with it, because you can no longer believe in God, who is everywhere present in it, then ask yourself, dear Mr Kappus, whether you have really lost God after all? Is it not rather the case that you have never yet possessed him? For when was it supposed to have been? Do you think a child can hold him, him whom grown men only bear with difficulty and whose weight bows down the old? Do you believe that anyone who really has him could lose him like a little pebble, or don't you think that whoever had him could only be lost by him alone? – But if you acknowledge that he was not present in your childhood, and not before that, if you suspect that Christ was deceived by his longing and Mohammed betrayed by his pride, and if you feel with horror that even now he is not present, at the moment when we are talking about him, what then gives you the right to miss him who never was, as if he had disappeared, and to search for him as if he were lost?

Why don't you think of him as a coming god, who since eternity has lain ahead of us, the future one, the eventual fruit of a tree of which we are the leaves? What prevents you from casting his birth out into the times of becoming and from living your life like a painful and beautiful day in the history of a great pregnancy? Don't you see how everything that happens is always a beginning again, and could it not be *His* beginning, given that beginnings are in themselves always so beautiful? If he is the complete being, must not slighter things come before him, so that he can pick himself out of fullness and abundance? – Must he not be the last in order to encompass all things in himself, and what significance would we have if the one whom we hanker for had already been?

As the bees collect honey together, so we fetch the sweetness out of everything and build *Him*. We begin with the very slightest things, with what is barely noticeable (as long as it comes about through love), with our work and the repose that comes after, with a moment of silence or with a small solitary joy, with everything that we do on our own without helpers and accomplices, we begin him whom we shall never know, just as our ancestors could not live to know us. And yet they are in us, these people long since passed away, as a disposition, as a load weighing on our destinies, as a murmur in the blood and as a gesture that rises up out of the depths of time.

Is there anything that can strip you of the hope of dwelling one day in him, the most remote, the most extreme?

Dear Mr Kappus, celebrate Christmas in the piety of the feeling that He perhaps requires of you precisely this existential anxiety in order to begin. Precisely these days of transition are perhaps the period when everything in you is working on him, just as before, as a child, you worked on him with bated breath. Be patient and even-tempered and remember that the least we can do is not make his becoming more difficult than the earth makes it for spring when it decides to come.

And I wish you happiness and confidence.

Yours,

Rainer Maria Rilke

Rome, 14 May 1904

My dear Mr Kappus,

Much time has gone past since I received your last letter. Don't hold that against me; first it was work, then disruptions and finally ill-health that kept me from replying, whereas I wanted to write to you out of good, peaceful days. Now I feel a little better again (even here the beginning of spring with its bad and fickle transitions was hard to bear) and can manage to send you greetings, dear Mr Kappus, and (as I am very glad to do) say this and that about your letter, as best I can.

You will see: I have copied out your sonnet because I found that it had beauty and simplicity and a native form in which it unfolds with such quiet propriety. It is the best of the verses of yours I have been permitted to read. And I'm giving you this copy now because I know that it is important and a whole new experience to come across a work of one's own in a foreign hand. Read the lines as if they were unknown to you, and you will feel in your inmost self how very much they are yours. –

It has been a pleasure for me to read this sonnet and your letter, which I did often. I thank you for both.

And you must not let yourself be diverted out of your solitude by the fact that something in you wants to escape from it. Precisely this desire, if you use it calmly and judiciously, as a kind of tool, will help you to extend your solitude over a greater expanse of ground. People have tended (with the help of conventions) to resolve everything in the direction of easiness, of the light, and on the lightest side of the light; but it is clear that we must hold to the heavy, the difficult. All living things do this, everything in nature grows and defends itself according to its kind and is a distinct creature from out of its own resources, strives to be so at any cost and in the face of all resistance. We know little, but that we must hold fast to what is difficult is a certainty that will never forsake us. It is good to be alone, for solitude is difficult; that something is difficult should be one more reason to do it.

To love is also good, for love is hard. Love between one person and another: that is perhaps the hardest thing it is laid on us to do, the utmost, the ultimate trial and test, the work for which all other work is just preparation. For this reason young people, who are beginners in everything, do not yet *know* how to love: they must learn. With their whole being, with all their strength, concerted on their solitary, fearful, upward beating hearts, they have to learn to love. An apprenticeship though is always a long, secluded period, and love too is for a great long time and far into life: solitariness, heightened and deepened loneliness for the one in love. Love at first has nothing to do with unfolding, abandon and uniting with another person (for what would be the sense in a union of what is unrefined and unfinished, still second order?);

for the individual it is a grand opportunity to mature, to become something in himself, to become a world, to become a world in himself for another's sake; it is a great immoderate demand made upon the self, something that singles him out and summons him to vast designs. Only in this sense, as a duty to work on themselves ('to hearken and to hammer day and night'), should young people use the love that is given them. The unfolding, the abandon and any kind of togetherness is not for them (who for a long time yet will have to scrimp and save). They are the culmination, and perhaps that for which a human life now is hardly sufficient.

But there young people so often and so badly go wrong: in that they (who by nature have no patience) fling themselves at one another when love comes over them, scatter themselves just as they are in all their troubledness, disorder, confusion . . . But what can come of that? What is life supposed to do with this heap of half-broken things that they call their togetherness and would like to call their happiness, were it possible, their future? Each person loses himself then for the other's sake and loses the other and many more who were yet to come. And loses the expanses and possibilities, exchanges the nearing and fleeing of delicate, mysterious things for a sterile helplessness of which nothing more can come; nothing but a bit of disgust, disappointment and deprivation and the escape into one of the many conventions which like public shelters are set up in great numbers along this most dangerous of paths. No area of human experience is so well furnished with conventions as this: there are lifebelts of the most various invention, dinghies and buoyancy devices; society in its wisdom has found ways of constructing refuges of all kinds, for since it has been disposed to make the love-life a pastime, it has also felt obliged to trivialize it, to make it cheap, risk-free and secure, as public pleasures usually are.

It is true that many young people who love wrongly, that is, simply with abandon and not in solitude (and your average person will never move beyond this), feel the oppression of having failed at something and do want to make the state into which they have got liveable and productive in their own, personal way; for their nature tells them that questions of love, even less than all other important matters, cannot be solved publicly and by following this or that consensus; that they are questions that touch the quick of what it is to be human and which in every case require a new, particular and *purely* private response: but how can people who have already flung together and no longer set themselves any limits or tell one another apart, and who therefore possess nothing of their own any more, how on earth can they find a way out of themselves, out of the depths of a solitude that has already been spilt and squandered?

They act out of a shared helplessness, and if they do their best to escape the convention they happen to have noticed (as marriage for example), they fall into the clutches of a less obvious but just as deadly conventional solution; for all around them there is nothing but – convention; when an action derives from a precipitately arrived at and unwitting union, it is *always* conventional; every relationship which is the product of such confusion has its conventions, however unusual (that is, immoral in the generally accepted sense) it may be; yes, even separation would in such a case be a conventional step, an impersonal, fortuitous decision without force and without point.

Whoever looks at the matter seriously finds that, as for death, which is difficult, no explanation, no solution, has yet been discovered for love, which is difficult too: there are no directions, no path. And for these two problems that we carry round with us in a sealed packet and hand on without opening, it will always be impossible to locate a common rule, resting on consensus. But to the same extent that we begin as individuals to venture onto life, these great things will encounter us, on our own, at ever closer quarters. The demands that the hard work of love makes on our development are larger than life, and as beginners we are not a match for them. But if we can hold out and take this love upon us as a burden and an apprenticeship, instead of losing ourselves in all the trivial and frivolous games behind which people have hidden from the utter seriousness of their existence, then perhaps a small advance and some relief will be sensible to those who come long after us. That would mean a great deal.

We are only now just coming to the point where we can consider the relationship of one human individual to another objectively and without prejudice, and our attempts to live such a relation have no model to go on. And yet in the shifting of the times there are already a few things that can help our tentative beginnings.

Girls and women, in their new, particular unfolding, will only in passing imitate men's behaviour and misbehaviour and follow in male professions. Once the uncertainty of such transitions is over it will emerge that women have only passed through the spectrum and the variety of those (often laughable) disguises in order to purify their truest natures from the distorting influences of the other sex. Women, in whom life abides and dwells more immediately, more fruitfully and more trustingly, are bound to have ripened more thoroughly, become more human human beings, than a man, who is all too light and has not been pulled down beneath the surface of life by the weight of a bodily fruit and who, in his arrogance and impatience, undervalues what he thinks he loves. This humanity which inhabits woman, brought to term in pain and humiliation, will, once she has shrugged off the conventions of mere femininity through the transformations of her outward status, come clearly to light, and men, who today do not yet feel it approaching, will be taken by surprise and struck down by it. One day (there are already reliable signs which speak for it and which begin to spread their light, especially in the northern countries), one day there will be girls and women whose name will no longer just signify the opposite of the male but something in their own right, something which does not make one think of any supplement or limit but only of life and existence: the female human being.

This step forward (at first right against the will of the men who are left behind) will transform the experience of love, which is now full of error, alter it root and branch, reshape it into a relation between two human beings and no longer between man and woman. And this more human form of love (which will be performed in infinitely gentle and considerate fashion, true and clear in its creating of bonds and dissolving of them) will resemble the one we are struggling and toiling to prepare the way for, the love that consists in two solitudes protecting, defining and welcoming one another.

And one more thing: do not believe that that abundance of love which was once, as a boy, bestowed on you is now lost. Can you tell whether back then great and good desires did not ripen within you, and resolutions which you still live by today? I believe that love remains so strong and powerful in your memory because it was your first deep experience of solitariness and the first inner work that you undertook on your life. – All good wishes to you, dear Mr Kappus!

Yours,

Rainer Maria Rilke

Sonnet

Through my life there trembles unlamenting
suffering dark and deep, without a sigh.
Pure as snow the blossoming of my dreams
consecrates the stillest of my days.

Often though a question's gravity
cuts across my path. I seem to shrink,
pass coldly on as if beside a lake
whose waters are too vast for me to measure.

And then a sadness settles, dim, opaque,
like the grey of pallid summer nights,
shimmered through with stars – now and then – :

love then is what my hands attempt to grasp
because I want to say a prayer whose sounds
my burning mouth, my lips, cannot bring forth . . .

(Franz Kappus)

Borgeby gård, Flădie, Sweden, 12 August 1904

I want to talk to you again for a while, dear Mr Kappus, although I can say almost nothing that is of any help, hardly anything useful. You have had many great sadnesses which have now passed by. And you say that their passing was also hard and upsetting for you. But I ask you to consider whether these great unhappinesses did not rather pass *through* you. Whether much within you has not changed, whether somewhere, in some part of your being, you were not transformed while you were unhappy? The only sorrows which are harmful and bad are those one takes among people in order to drown them out. Like diseases which are treated superficially and inexpertly, they only abate, and after a short pause break out again with more terrible force, and accumulate inside and are life, unlived, rejected, lost life – from which we can die. If it were possible for us to see further than our knowledge reaches, and a little beyond the outworks of our intuitions, perhaps we should then bear our sadnesses with greater assurance than our joys. For they are the moments when something new enters into us, something unknown to us; our feelings, shy and inhibited, fall silent, everything in us withdraws, a stillness settles on us, and at the centre of it is the new presence that nobody yet knows, making no sound.

I believe that almost all our sadnesses are periods of tautening that we experience as numbness because we can no longer hear the stirring of our feelings, which have become foreign to us. Because we are alone with the strange thing that has entered into us; because everything familiar and accustomed is taken away from us for a moment; because we are in the middle of a transition where we cannot stand still. And that is why sadness passes: what is new in us, the thing that has supervened, has entered into our heart, penetrated to its innermost chamber and not lingered even there – it is already in our blood. And we never quite know what it was. One might easily suppose that nothing had happened, but we have altered the way a house alters when a guest enters it. We cannot say who has come, perhaps we shall never know, but there are many indications that it is the future that enters into us like this, in order to be transformed within us, long before it actually occurs. And that is why it is so important to be solitary and attentive when one is sad: because the apparently uneventful and static moment when our future comes upon us is so much closer to life than that other noisy and accidental point when it happens to us as if from the outside. The quieter, the more patient and open we are in our sadness, the deeper and more unerringly the new will penetrate into us, the better we shall acquire it, the more it will be *our* fate, and when one day in the future it 'takes place' (that is, steps out of us towards others) we shall feel related and close to it in our inmost hearts. And that is necessary. It is necessary – and little by little our development will tend in this direction – that nothing alien should happen to us, but only what has long been part of us. We have already had to adjust our understanding of so many theories of planetary motion, and so too we shall gradually learn to recognize that what we call fate originates in ourselves, in humankind, and does not work on us from the outside. Only because so many people did not absorb their fates while they were inhabited by them, and did not make them a part of themselves, only because of this did they fail to recognize what emerged from them. It was so foreign to them that in their confused panic they assumed it must just have entered into them, for they swore never to have found anything of the sort in themselves before. Just as for a long time people were deceived about the movement of the sun, so we are still deceived about the movement of what is to come. The future is fixed, dear Mr Kappus, but we move around in infinite space.

How could things not be difficult for us?

And if we come back to solitude, it grows ever clearer that fundamentally it is not something that one can take or leave. We *are* solitary. It is possible to deceive yourself and act as if it were not the case. That is all. How much better though, to see and accept that that is what we are, and even to take it as our starting-point. If we do, the effect is admittedly one of giddiness; for all the points on which we are accustomed to rest our eyes are taken away from us, there is no longer anything close by, and everything remote is infinitely so. Someone transported from his room, almost without warning and interval, onto the top of a high mountain would feel something like it: he would be virtually destroyed by an unparalleled sense of insecurity, by an exposure to something nameless. He would think he was falling or believe himself to be hurtling out into space or shattered into a thousand pieces: what a monstrous lie his brain would have to invent to rein in and clarify the state of his senses. In the same way all distances, all measurements, alter for the one who becomes solitary; many such changes suddenly take place at once and, as with the man on the mountaintop, unusual imaginings and curious sensations occur which seem to take on dimensions greater than can be tolerated. But it is necessary for us to experience this too. We must accept our existence in as *wide* a sense as can be; everything, even the unheard-of, must be possible within it. That, when you come down to it, is the only kind of courage that is demanded of us: the courage for the oddest, the most unexpected, the most inexplicable things that we may encounter. That human beings have been cowardly in this regard has done life endless harm; the experiences we describe as 'apparitions', the entire so-called 'spirit world', death, all those things so closely akin to us have by our daily rejection of them been forced so far out of our lives that the senses with which we might apprehend them have atrophied. To say nothing of God. But the fear of the inexplicable has not just rendered the individual existence poorer; relations *between* people, too, have been restricted, as it were lifted out of the river-bed of endless possibilities and placed on a deserted bank where nothing happens. For it is not lethargy alone which causes human relationships to repeat themselves in the same old way with such unspeakable monotony in instance after instance; it is the fearful shying away from any kind of new, unforeseeable experience which we think we may not be equal to. But only someone who is ready for anything and rules nothing out, not even the most enigmatic things, will experience the relationship with another as a living thing and will himself live his own existence to the full. For imagining an individual's existence as a larger or smaller room reveals to us that most people are only acquainted with one corner of their particular room, a place by the window, a little area to pace up and down. That way, they have a certain security. And yet the perilous uncertainty that drives the prisoners in Poe's tales to grope out the outlines of their terrible dungeons and so to know the unspeakable horrors of their surroundings, is so much more human. But we are not prisoners. There are no traps or snares set up around us, and there is nothing that should frighten or torment us. We are placed into life as into the element with which we have the most affinity, and moreover we have after thousands of years of adaptation come to resemble this life so closely that if we keep still we can, thanks to our facility for mimicry, hardly be distinguished from all that surrounds us. We have no reason to be mistrustful of our world, for it is not against us. If it holds terrors they are *our* terrors, if it has its abysses these abysses belong to us, if there are dangers then we must try to love them. And if we only organize our life according to the principle which teaches us always to hold to what is difficult, then what now still appears most foreign will become our most intimate and most reliable experience. How can we forget those ancient myths found at the beginnings of all peoples? The myths about the dragons who at the last moment turn into princesses? Perhaps all the dragons in our lives are princesses, only waiting for the day when they will see us handsome and brave? Perhaps everything terrifying is deep down a helpless thing that needs our help.

So, dear Mr Kappus, you shouldn't be dismayed if a sadness rises up in front of you, greater than any you have ever seen before; or if a disquiet plays over your hands and over all your doings like light and cloud-shadow. You must think that something is happening with you, that life has not forgotten you, that it holds you in its hand; it will not let you fall. Why should you want to exclude from your life all unsettling, all pain, all depression of spirit, when you don't know what work it is these states are performing within you? Why do you want to persecute yourself with the question of where it all comes from and where it is leading? You well know you are in a period of transition and want nothing more than to be transformed. If there is something ailing in the way you go about things, then remember that sickness is the means by which an organism rids itself of something foreign to it. All one has to do is help it to be ill, to have its whole illness and let it break out, for that is how it mends itself. There is so much, my dear Mr Kappus, going on in you now. You must be patient as an invalid and trusting as a convalescent, for you are perhaps both. And more than that: you are also the doctor responsible for looking after himself. But with all illnesses there are many days when the doctor can do nothing but wait. And inasfar as you are your own doctor, this above all is what you must do now.

Do not watch yourself too closely. Do not draw over-rapid conclusions from what is happening to you. Simply let it happen. Otherwise you will too readily find yourself looking on your past, which is of course not uninvolved with everything that is going on in you now, reproachfully (that is, moralistically). But what now affects you from among the divagations, desires and longings of your boyhood is not what you will recall and condemn. The extraordinary circumstances of a solitary and helpless childhood are so difficult, so complicated, exposed to so many influences and at the same time removed from any real life-context, that if a vice enters into it we must not be too quick to call it a vice. We should in general be very careful with names; it is so often the name of a crime which destroys a life, not the nameless and personal act itself, which was perhaps completely necessary to that life and could have been absorbed by it without difficulty. And the expenditure of energy only seems so great because you put too much importance on the victory. It is not victory that is the 'great thing' you think you have achieved, though the feeling itself is not in error. What is great is that there was already something there that you were able to set in place of that deception, something true and real. Without it, your victory would only have been a moral reaction with no further significance, but as it is it has become a segment of your life. Of your life, dear Mr Kappus, which I am thinking of with so many hopes and wishes. Do you remember how this life of yours longed in childhood to belong to the 'grown-ups'? I can see that it now longs to move on from them and is drawn to those who are greater yet. That is why it does not cease to be difficult, but also why it will not cease to grow.

And if I have anything else to say to you it is this: do not think that the person who is trying to console you lives effortlessly among the simple, quiet words that sometimes make you feel better. His life is full of troubles and sadness and falls far short of them. But if it were any different he could never have found the words that he did.

Yours,

Rainer Maria Rilke

Furuborg, Jonsered, Sweden, 4 November 1904

My dear Mr Kappus,

During this time that has passed without a letter I was partly travelling and partly too busy to be able to write. And even today writing is not going to be easy because I have had to write a good number of letters already and my hand is tired. If I had someone to dictate to I'd have plenty to say, but as it is you'll have to make do with just a few words in return for your long letter.

I think of you often, dear Mr Kappus, and with such a concentration of good wishes that really in some way it ought to help. Whether my letters can really be a help to you, well, I have my doubts. Do not say: Yes, they are. Just let them sink in quietly and without any particular sense of gratitude, and let's wait and see what will come of it.

There's not perhaps much purpose in my dealing with the detail of what you wrote, for what I might be able to say about your tendency towards self-doubt or your inability to reconcile your inner and outer life, or about anything else that assails you – it all comes down to what I have said before: the same desire that you might find enough patience in you to endure, and simplicity enough to have faith; that you might gain more and more trust in what is hard and in your own loneliness among other people. And otherwise let life take its course. Believe me: life is right, whatever happens.

And as to feelings: all feelings are pure that focus you and raise you up. An impure feeling is one that only comprises *one* side of your nature and so distorts you. Any thoughts that match up to your childhood are good. Everything that makes *more* of you than you have hitherto been in your best moments is right. Every heightening is good if it occurs in the quick of your bloodstream, if it is not an intoxication, not a troubling but a joy one can see right to the bottom of. Do you understand what I mean?

And your doubts can become a good quality if you *school* them. They must grow to be *knowledgeable*, they must learn to be critical. As soon as they begin to spoil something for you ask them *why* a thing is ugly, demand hard evidence, test them, and you will perhaps find them at a loss and short of an answer, or perhaps mutinous. But do not give in, request arguments, and act with this kind of attentiveness and consistency every single time, and the day will come when instead of being demolishers they will be among your best workers – perhaps the canniest of all those at work on the building of your life.

That is all, dear Mr Kappus, that I can say to you for today. But I'm also sending you the off-print of a little work that has just appeared in the Prague journal *Deutsche Arbeit*. There I continue to speak to you of life and of death and of the greatness and splendour of both.

Yours,

Rainer Maria Rilke

Paris, on the second day of Christmas 1908

You ought to know, dear Mr Kappus, how happy I was to get this lovely letter from you. The news you give me, actual and articulate as it now is, seems good to me, and the more I thought about it the more it struck me as incontrovertibly good. I really wanted to write you this in time for Christmas Eve; but what with the work that has been occupying me variously and without interruption this winter the old festival came up so quickly that I hardly had time enough to make the most necessary purchases, much less to write a letter.

But during these Christmas days I have often thought of you and imagined how quiet you must be in your solitary fort up among the empty mountains over which those great south winds rush as if they wanted to devour them in mighty chunks.

The silence must be immense to be able to receive such sounds and movements, and when one thinks that they are joined by the noise of the sea, present in the distance, perhaps the most inward note in this prehistoric harmony, one can only hope that you have the trust and patience to let this marvellous solitude work on you, a solitude which will never be deleted from your life. In all that lies before you to experience and do, it will continue as an anonymous influence and have a subtly decisive effect, perhaps like the way the blood of our ancestors moves unceasingly within us and mingles with our own to make us the unique, not-to-be-repeated being that we are at every turn of our lives.

Yes: I am glad that you have this firm, utterable form of existence, the rank, the uniform, the duty, all these tangible and well-defined things that in such surroundings, with an equally isolated and not numerous company of men, take on a seriousness and necessity; and which, over and above the aspects of play and pastime that are also part of the military profession, make for a certain vigilance and not only permit an individual attentiveness but actually teach it. And to be in circumstances that work on us, that set us before great natural phenomena from time to time, is all we need.

Art too is only a way of living, and it is possible, however one lives, to prepare oneself for it without knowing; in every real situation we are nearer to it, better neighbours, than in the unreal half-artistic professions which by pretending to be close to art in fact deny and hurt its very existence, as for example is the case with the whole of journalism and almost all criticism and three-quarters of what passes for literature. I am glad, in a word, that you have withstood the dangers of slipping into all this, and that somewhere you are living alone and courageous in a rough reality. May the year to come maintain and strengthen you in it.

Ever yours,

R. M. Rilke

Penguin Little Black Classics Vol. I

01. GIOVANNI BOCCACCIO
Mrs Rosie and the Priest

02. EDGAR ALLAN POE
The Tell-Tale Heart

03. ANTON CHEKHOV
Gooseberries

04. LEO TOLSTOY
How Much Land Does a Man Need?

05. GUSTAVE FLAUBERT
A Simple Heart

06. RYUNOSUKE AKUTAGAWA
The Life of a Stupid Man

07. THOMAS HARDY
The Withered Arm

08. KENKO
A Cup of Sake Beneath the Cherry Trees

09. WILLIAM BLAKE
Tyger Tyger

10. RAINER MARIA RILKE
Letters to a Young Poet

企鹅经典：小黑书　第一辑

01. 贝尔科洛蕾夫人与神父

[意] 薄伽丘

02. 泄密的心

[美] 爱伦·坡

03. 醋栗

[俄] 契诃夫

04. 一个人需要许多土地吗？

[俄] 列夫·托尔斯泰

05. 一颗简单的心

[法] 福楼拜

06. 傻子的一生

[日] 芥川龙之介

07. 萎缩的胳膊

[英] 托马斯·哈代

08. 樱花树下的清酒

[日] 吉田兼好

09. 虎！虎！

[英] 威廉·布莱克

10. 给一个青年诗人的十封信

[奥] 里尔克

“一切都要亲身生活。
现在你就在这些问题里
‘生活’吧。”

PENGUIN

LITTLE BLACK

CLASSICS

*此中文译本译自德语原文

给一个青年诗人的十封信

Letters to a Young Poet

[奥] 里尔克 著

冯至 译

中信出版集团 · 北京

图书在版编目（C I P）数据

企鹅经典 · 小黑书 . 第一辑 : 英、汉 / (日) 吉田兼好等著 ; 文东等译 . -- 北京 : 中信出版社 , 2018.11 (2022.7 重印)
书名原文 : Penguin Little Black Classics
ISBN 978-7-5086-9400-9

Ⅰ . ①企… Ⅱ . ①吉… ②文… Ⅲ . ①世界文学一作品综合集一英、汉 Ⅳ . ① I11

中国版本图书馆 CIP 数据核字 (2018) 第 193780 号

Letters to a Young Poet
Letters to a Young Poet was first published in 1929. This edition is taken from Letters to a Young Poet & The Letter from the Young Worker translated by Charlie Louth, Penguin Classics, 2011. This selection published in Penguin Classics 2016. Translation copyright © Charlie Louth, 2011. The moral right of the translator has been asserted.
Simplified Chinese translation copyright © 冯至 . All rights reserved.

本书仅限中国大陆地区发行销售

® “企鹅”及其相关标识是企鹅图书有限公司已经注册或尚未注册的商标。
未经允许，不得擅用。
封底凡无企鹅防伪标识者均属未经授权之非法版本。

企鹅经典：小黑书　第一辑
给一个青年诗人的十封信

著　　者：[奥] 里尔克
译　　者：冯 至
出版发行：中信出版集团股份有限公司
（北京市朝阳区惠新东街甲 4 号富盛大厦 2 座 邮编 100029）
承 印 者：河北鹏润印刷有限公司

开　　本：787mm×1092mm　1/32　　印　　张：41　　字　　数：300 千字
版　　次：2018 年 11 月第 1 版　　印　　次：2022 年 7 月第13次印刷
京权图字：01-2018-6477
书　　号：ISBN 978-7-5086-9400-9
定　　价：149.00 元（全 10 册）

版权所有 · 侵权必究
如有印刷、装订问题，本公司负责调换。
服务热线：400-600-8099
投稿邮箱：author@citicpub.com

目录

译者序

这十封信是赖内·马利亚·里尔克（Rainer Maria Rilke，1875—1926）在他三十岁左右时写给一个青年诗人的。里尔克除却他诗人的天职外，还是一个永不疲倦的书简家；他一生写过无数比这十封更亲切、更美的信。但是这十封信却浑然天成，无形中自有首尾；向着青年说得最多。里边他论到诗和艺术，论到两性的爱，严肃和冷嘲，悲哀和怀疑，论到生活和职业的艰难——这都是青年人心里时常起伏的问题。

人们爱把青年比作春，这比喻是正确的。可是彼此的相似点与其说是青年人的晴朗有如春阳的明丽，倒不如从另一方面看，青年人的愁苦、青年人的生长，更像那在

阴云暗淡的风里、雨里、寒里演变着的春。因为后者比前者更漫长、沉重而更有意义。我时常在任何一个青年的面前，便联想起荷兰画家梵·高的一幅题作《春》的画：那幅画背景是几所矮小、狭窄的房屋，中央立着一棵桃树或杏树，杈丫的枝干上寂寞地开着几朵粉红色的花。我想，这棵树是经过了长期的风雨，如今还在忍受着春寒，四围是一个穷乏的世界，在枝干内却流动着生命的汁浆。这是一个真实的、没有夸耀的春天！青年人又何尝不是这样呢，生命无时不需要生长，而外边却不永远是日光和温暖的风。他们要担当许多的寒冷和无情、淡漠和误解。他们一切都充满了新鲜的生气，而社会的习俗却是腐旧的，腐旧得像是洗染了许多遍的衣衫。他们觉得内心和外界无法协调，处处受着限制，同时又不能像植物似的那样沉默，他们要向人告诉——他们寻找能够听取他们的话的人，他们寻找能从他们表现力不很充足的话里体会出他们的本意而给以解答的过来人。在这样的寻找中几乎是一百个青年有一百个失望了。但是有一人，本来是一时的兴会，写出一封抒发自己内心状况的信，寄给一个不相识的诗人，那诗人读完了信有所会心，想起自己的青少年时代，仿佛在抚摸他过去身上的伤痕，随即来一封，回答一封，对于每个问题

都给一个精辟的回答和分析——同时他却一再声明，人人都要自己料理，旁人是很难给以一些帮助的。

可是他告诉我们，人到世上来，是艰难而孤单。一个个的人在世上好似园里的那些并排着的树。枝枝叶叶也许有些呼应吧，但是它们的根，它们盘结在地下摄取营养的根却各不相干，又沉静，又孤单。人每每为了无谓的喧嚣，忘却生命的根蒂，不能在寂寞中、在对草木鸟兽（它们和我们一样都是生物）的观察中体验一些生的意义，只在人生的表面上永远往下滑过去。这样，自然无所谓艰难，也无所谓孤单，只是隐瞒和欺骗。欺骗和隐瞒的工具，里尔克告诉我们说，是社会的习俗。人在遇见了艰难，遇见了恐怖，遇见了严重的事物而无法应付时，便会躲在习俗的下边去求它的庇护。它成了人们的避难所，却不是安身立命的地方——谁若是要真实地生活，就必须脱离开现成的习俗，自己独立成为一个生存者，担当生活上种种的问题，和我们的始祖所担当过的一样，不能容有一些儿代替。

在这几封信里，处处流露着这种意义，使读者最受感动。当我于 1931 年的春天，第一次读到这一小册书信时，觉得字字都好似从自己心里流出来，又流回到自己心里，感到一种满足，一种兴奋，禁不住读完一封，便翻译一封，

为的是寄给不能读德文的远方的朋友。如今已经过了六年，原书不知又重版多少次，而我的译稿则在行箧内睡了几年觉，始终没有印成书。现在我把它取出来，略加修改付印，仍然是献给不能读德文原文的朋友。

关于里尔克的一生和他的著作，不能在这短短的序中有所叙述。去年他去世十周年纪念时，上海的《新诗》月刊第一卷第三期，曾为他出了一个特辑，读者可以参看。他的作品有一部分已由卞之琳、梁宗岱、冯至译成中文，散见《沉钟》半月刊、《华胥社论文集》、《新诗》月刊、大公报的《文艺》和《艺术周刊》中。

至于收信人的身世，我知道得很少，大半正如他的《引言》上所说的一样，后来生活把他“赶入了正是这位诗人温暖、和蔼而多情的关怀”所为他“防护的境地”了。

1937 年 5 月 1 日

收信人引言

1902 年的深秋——我在维也纳·新城陆军学校的校园里，坐在古老的栗树下读着一本书。我读时是这样专心，几乎没有注意到，那位在我们学校中唯一不是军官的教授、博学而慈祥的校内牧师荷拉捷克（Horaček）是怎样走近我的身边。他从我的手里取去那本书，看看封面，摇摇头。“赖内·马利亚·里尔克的诗？”他深思着问。随后他翻了几页，读了几行，望着远方出神，最后才点头说道：“勒内·里尔克[1]从陆军学生变成一个诗人了。”

---

1. 里尔克少年时名勒内·里尔克（René Rilke）。（说明：书中脚注均为译者注。）

于是我知道一些关于这个瘦弱苍白的儿童的事，十五年前他的父母希望他将来做军官，把他送到圣坡尔腾（Sankt-Pölten）的陆军初级学校读书。那时荷拉捷克在那里当牧师，他还能清清楚楚想得起这个陆军学生。他说他是一个平静、严肃、天资很高的少年，喜欢寂寞，忍受着宿舍生活的压抑，四年后跟别的学生一齐升入梅里史·外司克尔心（Mäbrisch-Weisskirchen）地方的陆军高级中学。可是他的体格担受不起，于是他的父母把他从学校里召回，教他在故乡布拉格继续读书。此后他的生活怎样发展，荷拉捷克就不知道了。

按照这一切很容易了解，这时我立即决定把我的诗的试作寄给赖内·马利亚·里尔克，请他批评。我还没有满二十岁，就逼近一种职业的门槛，我正觉得这职业与我的意趣相违，我希望，如果向旁人去寻求理解，就不如向这位《自庆》[1]的作者去寻求了。我无意中在寄诗时还附加一封信，信上自述是这样坦白，我在这以前和以后从不曾向第二个人做过。

几个星期过去，回信来了。信上印着巴黎的戳记，

1.《自庆》（*Mir zur Feier*），里尔克早年的诗集，1899 年出版。

握在手里很沉重；从头至尾写着与信封上同样清晰美丽而固定的字体。于是我同赖内·马利亚·里尔克开始了不断的通信，继续到 1908 年才渐渐稀疏，因为生活把我赶入了正是诗人的温暖、和蔼而多情的关怀所为我防护的境地。

这些事并不重要。所重要的是下边的这十封信，为了理解里尔克所生活所创造的世界是重要的，为了今日和明天许多生长者和完成者也是重要的。一个伟大的人、旷百世而一遇的人说话的地方，小人物必须沉默。

弗兰斯·克萨危尔·卡卜斯

(Franz Xaver Kappus)

1929 年 6 月，柏林

第一封信

尊敬的先生:

你的信前几天才转到我这里。我要感谢你信里博大而亲爱的信赖。此外我能做的事很少。我不能评论你的诗艺；因为每个批评的意图都离我太远。再没有比批评的文字那样同一件艺术品隔膜的了；同时总是演出来较多或较少的凑巧的误解。一切事物都不是像人们要我们相信的那样可言传的，它们完全在一个语言从未达到过的空间；可是比一切更不可言传的是艺术品，它们是神秘的生存，它们的生命在我们无常的生命之外赓续着。

我既然预先写出这样的意见，可是我还得向你说，你的诗没有自己的特点，自然暗中也静静地潜伏着向着

个性发展的趋势。我感到这种情形最明显的是在最后一首《我的灵魂》里，这首诗字里行间显示出一些自己的东西。还有那首优美的诗《给雷渥琶地》[1]也洋溢着一种同这位伟大而寂寞的诗人精神上的契合。虽然如此，你的诗本身还不能算什么，还不是独立的，就是那最后的一首和《给雷渥琶地》也不是。我读你的诗感到有些不能明确说出的缺陷，可是你随诗寄来的亲切的信，却把这些缺陷无形中给我说明了。

你在信里问你的诗好不好。你问我。你从前也问过别人。你把它们寄给杂志。你把你的诗跟别人的比较；若是某些编辑部退回了你的试作，你就不安。那么（因为你允许我向你劝告），我请你，把这一切放弃吧！你向外看，是你现在最不应该做的事。没有人能给你出主意，没有人能够帮助你。只有一个唯一的方法。请你走向内心。探索那叫你写的缘由，考察它的根是不是盘在你心的深处；你要坦白承认，万一你写不出来，是不是必得因此而死去。这是最重要的——在你夜深最寂静的时刻问问自己：我必须写吗？你要在自身内挖掘一个深

1. 雷渥琶地（Giacomo Leopardi，1798—1837），意大利著名诗人。

的答复。若是这个答复表示同意，而你也能够以一种坚强、单纯的“我必须”来对答那个严肃的问题，那么，你就根据这个需要去建造你的生活吧；你的生活直到它最寻常最细琐的时刻，都必须是这个创造冲动的标志和证明。然后你接近自然。你要像一个原人似的练习去说你所见、所体验、所爱以及所遗失的事物。不要写爱情诗，先要回避那些太流行、太普通的格式：它们是最难的，因为那里聚有大量好的或是一部分精美的流传下来的作品，从中再表现出自己的特点则需要一种巨大而熟练的力量。所以你要躲开那些普遍的题材，而归依于你自己日常生活呈现给你的事物；你描写你的悲哀与愿望，流逝的思想与对于某一种美的信念——用深幽、寂静、谦虚的真诚描写这一切，用你周围的事物、梦中的图影、回忆中的对象表现自己。如果你觉得你的日常生活很贫乏，你不要抱怨它；还是怨你自己吧，怨你还不够做一个诗人来呼唤生活的宝藏，因为对于创造者没有贫乏，也没有贫瘠不关痛痒的地方。即使你自己是在一座监狱里，狱墙使人世间的喧嚣和你的官感隔离——你不还永远据有你的童年吗，这贵重的富丽的宝藏，回忆的宝库？你往那方面多多用心吧！试行拾捡起过去久已消

沉了的动人的往事；你的个性将渐渐固定，你的寂寞将渐渐扩大，成为一所朦胧的住室，别人的喧扰只远远地从旁走过——如果从这收视反听，从这向自己世界的深处产生出“诗”来，你一定不会再想问别人，这是不是好诗。你也不会再尝试让杂志去注意这些作品，因为你将在作品里看到你亲爱的天然产物，你生活的断片与声音。一件艺术品是好的，只要它是从“必要”里产生的。在它这样的根源里就含有对它的评判：别无他途。所以，尊敬的先生，除此以外我也没有别的劝告：走向内心，探索你生活发源的深处，在它的发源处你将会得到问题的答案，是不是“必须”创造。它怎么说，你怎么接受，不必加以说明。它也许告诉你，你的职责是艺术家。那么你就接受这个命运，承担起它的重负和伟大，不要关心从外边来的报酬。因为创造者必须自己是一个完整的世界，在自身和自身所联接的自然界里得到一切。

但也许经过一番向自己、向寂寞的探索之后，你就断念做一个诗人了（那也够了，感到自己不写也能够生活时，就可以使我们决然不再去尝试）；就是这样，我向你所请求的反思也不是徒然的。无论如何，你的生活将从此寻得自己的道路，并且那该是良好、丰富、广阔的

道路，我所愿望于你的比我所能说出的多得多。

我还应该向你说什么呢？我觉得一切都本其自然；归结我也只是这样劝你，静静地严肃地从你的发展中成长起来；没有比向外看和从外面等待回答会更严重地伤害你的发展了，你要知道，你的问题也许只是你最深的情感在你最微妙的时刻所能回答的。

我很高兴，在你的信里见到了荷拉捷克教授的名字；我对于这位亲切的学者怀有很大的敬意和多年不变的感激。请你替我向他致意；他至今还记得我，我实在引为荣幸。

你盛意寄给我的诗，现奉还。我再一次感谢你对我信赖的博大与忠诚；我本来是个陌生人，不能有所帮助，但我要通过这封本着良知写的忠实的回信报答你的依赖于万一。

以一切的忠诚与关怀：

赖内·马利亚·里尔克

1903 年 2 月 18 日，巴黎

第二封信

／

请你原谅我，亲爱的、尊敬的先生，我直到今天才感谢地想到你 2 月 24 日的来信：这段时间我很苦恼，不是病，但是一种流行性感冒类的衰弱困扰我做什么事都没有力气。最后，这种现象一点也没变，我才来到这曾经疗养过我一次的南方的海滨。但是我还未康复，写作还困难，你只得接受这封短信代替我更多的心意。

你自然必须知道，你的每封信都永远使我欢喜，可是你要宽恕我的回答，它也许对你没有什么帮助；因为在根本处，也正是在那最深奥、最重要的事物上我们是无名地孤单；要是一个人能够对别人劝告，甚至帮助时，彼此间必须有许多事情实现了，完成了，一切事物必须

有一个完整的安排，才会有一次的效验。

今天我只要向你谈两件事：第一是“暗嘲”（Ironie）[1]：

你不要让你被它支配，尤其是在创造力贫乏的时刻。在创造力丰富的时候你可以试行运用它，当作一种方法去理解人生。纯洁地用，它就是纯洁的，不必因为它而感到羞愧；如果你觉得你同它过于亲密，又怕同它的亲密日见增长，那么你就转向伟大、严肃的事物吧，在它们面前它会变得又渺小又可怜。寻求事物的深处：在深处暗嘲是走不下去的——若是你把它引近伟大的边缘，你应该立即考量这个理解的方式（暗嘲）是不是发自你本性的一种需要。因为在严肃事物的影响下（如果它是偶然发生的），它会脱离了你（如果它真是天生就属于你），它就会强固成为一个严正的工具，而列入你创作艺术的一些方法的行列中。

第二件我今天要向你说的是：

在我所有的书中只有少数的几本是不能离身的，有两部书甚至无论我走到哪里都在我的行囊里。此刻它们也在我的身边：一部是《圣经》，一部是丹麦伟大

1.Ironie，一译“反讽”。

诗人茵斯·彼得·雅阔布生[1]的书。我忽然想起，不知你读过他的著作没有。这很容易买到，因为有一部分很好的翻译在雷克拉木（Reclam）万有文库中出版。你去买他的《六篇短篇小说》和他的长篇《尼尔·律内》（Niels Lyhne）。你先读前一本的第一篇《摩根斯》（Mogens）。一个世界将要展现在你的面前，一个世界的幸福、丰富、不可捉摸的伟大。请你在这两本书里体验一些时，学你以为值得学的事物，但最重要的是你要爱它们。这种爱将为你得到千千万万的回报，并且，无论你的生活取怎样的途径——我确信它将穿过你的成长的丝纶，在你一切经验、失望与欢悦的线索中成为最重要的一条。

如果我应该说，从谁那里我体验到一些关于创作的本质以及它的深奥与它的永恒的意义，那么我只能说出两个名字：一个是雅阔布生，伟大的诗人；一个是奥古斯特·罗丹[2]，那在现存的艺术家中无人能与比拟

---

1. 茵斯·彼得·雅阔布生（Jens Peter Jacobsen，1847—1885），丹麦小说家、诗人，著有长、短篇小说及诗、随笔等。
2. 奥古斯特·罗丹（Auguste Rodin，1840—1917），法国雕刻家，里尔克于 1902 年赴巴黎，拜访罗丹，于 1906 年曾短期任罗丹秘书。

的雕刻家。

愿你前途一切成功！

你的：赖内·马利亚·里尔克

1903 年 4 月 5 日，意大利

比萨（Pisa），维亚雷焦（Viareggio）

第三封信

亲爱的、尊敬的先生，你复活节的来信给我许多欢喜；因为它告诉我许多关于你的好消息，并且像你对雅阔布生伟大而可爱的艺术所抒发的意见也可以证明，我把你的生活和生活上的许多问题引到这丰富的世界里来，我并没有做错。

现在你该读《尼尔·律内》了，那是一部壮丽而深刻的书；越读越好像一切都在书中，从生命最轻妙的芬芳到它沉重的果实的厚味。这里没有一件事不能被我们去理解、领会、经验，以及在回忆的余韵中亲切地认识；没有一种体验是过于渺小的，就是很小的事件的开展都像是一个大的命运，并且这命运本身像是一块奇异的广

大的织物，每条线都被一只无限温柔的手引来，排在另一条线的旁边，千百条互相持衡。你将要得到首次读这本书时的大幸福，通过无数意料不到的惊奇仿佛在一个新的梦里。可是我能够向你说，往后我们读这些书时永远是个惊讶者，它们永不能失去它们的魅力，连它们首次给予读者的童话的境界也不会失掉。

我们只在那些书中享受日深，感激日笃，观察更为明确而单纯，对于生的信仰更为深沉，在生活里也更幸福博大——

往后你要读那部叙述马丽·葛鲁伯夫人的命运与渴望的奇书[1]，还有雅阔布生的信札、日记、片断，最后还有他的诗（纵使是平庸的德文翻译），也自有不能磨灭的声韵（这时我要劝告你，遇机会时可以去买一部雅阔布生的全集，一切都在里边。共三册，译文很好，莱比锡外根·笛得利许（Eugen Diederichs）书店出版，每册据我所知只卖五六个马克）。

关于那篇非常细腻而精练的短篇小说《这里该有蔷薇……》，你对于作序者不同的意见实在很对。顺便我劝

1. 指雅阔布生的长篇小说《马丽·葛鲁伯夫人》(*Frau Marie Crubbe*)。

你尽可能少读审美批评的文字——它们多半是一偏之见，已经枯僵在没有生命的硬化中，毫无意义；不然就是乖巧地卖弄笔墨，今天这派得势，明天又是相反的那派。艺术品都是源于无穷的寂寞，没有比批评更难望其边际的了。只有爱能够理解它们，把住它们，认识它们的价值——面对每个这样的说明、评论或导言，你要相信你自己和你的感觉；万一你错误了，你内在的生命自然的成长会慢慢地随时使你认识你的错误，把你引到另外的一条路上。让你的判断力静静地发展，发展跟每个进步一样，是深深地从内心出来，既不能强迫，也不能催促。一切都是时至才能产生。让每个印象与一种情感的萌芽在自身里、在暗中、在不能言说，不知不觉、个人理解所不能达到的地方完成。以深深的谦虚与忍耐去期待一个新的豁然贯通的时刻：这才是艺术地生活，无论是理解或是创造，都一样。

不能计算时间，年月都无效，就是十年有时也等于虚无。艺术家是：不算，不数；像树木似的成熟，不勉强挤它的汁液，满怀信心地立在春日的暴风雨中，也不担心后边没有夏天来到。夏天终归是会来的。但它只向着忍耐的人们走来；他们在这里，好像永恒总在他们面前，

无忧无虑地寂静而广大。我天天学习，在我所感谢的痛苦中学习：“忍耐”是一切！

谈到理洽特·德美尔[1]：他的书（同时也可以说他这个人，我泛泛地认识他），我觉得是这样，每逢我读到他的一页好诗时，我常常怕读到第二页，又把前边的一切破坏，将可爱之处变得索然无味。你把他的性格刻画得很对：“情欲地生活，情欲地创作。”——其实艺术家的体验是这样不可思议地接近于性的体验，接近于它的痛苦与它的快乐，这两种现象本来只是同一渴望与幸福的不同的形式。若是可以不说是“情欲”——而说是“性”，是博大的、纯洁的、没有被教会的谬误所诋毁的意义中的“性”，那么他的艺术或者会很博大而永久地重要。他诗人的力是博大的，坚强似一种原始的冲动，在他自身内有勇往直前的韵律爆发出来，像是从雄浑的山中。

但我觉得，这个力并不永远是完全直率的，不无装腔作态（这对于创造者实在是一个严峻的考验，他必须永远不曾意识到、不曾预感到他最好的美德，如果他要保持住那美德的自然而混元的境地）。现在这个鼓动着他

1. 理洽特·德美尔（Richard Dehmel，1863—1920），德国诗人，当时享有盛名。

的本性的力向性的方面进发，但是它却没有找到它所需要的那个纯洁的人。那里没有一个成熟而纯洁的性的世界，只有一个缺乏广泛的“人性”，而只限于“男性”的世界，充满了情欲、迷醉与不安，为男人旧日的成见与傲慢的心所累，使爱失却了本来的面目。因为他只是作为男人去爱，不是作为人去爱，所以在他的性的感觉中有一些狭窄、粗糙、仇恨、无常，没有永久性的成分存在，减低艺术的价值，使艺术支离晦涩。这样的艺术不会没有污点，它被时代与情欲所渲染，很少能持续存在（多数的艺术却都是这样）。虽然，我们也可以享受其中一些卓绝的地方，可是不要沉溺迷失，变成德美尔世界中的信徒；他的世界是这样无穷地烦恼，充满了奸情、迷乱，同真实的命运距离太远了；真实的命运比起这些暂时的忧郁使人更多地担受痛苦，但也给人以更多的机会走向伟大，更多的勇气向着永恒。

最后关于我的书，我很愿意送你一整份你所喜欢的。但我很穷，并且我的书一出版就不属于我了。我自己不能买，虽然我常常想赠给能够对于我的书表示爱好的人们。

所以我在另纸上写给你我最近出版的书名和出版的书局（只限于最近的；若是算上从前的共有十二三种），亲

爱的先生，我把这书单给你，遇机会时你任意订购好了。

我愿意我的书在你的身边。

珍重！

你的：赖内·马利亚·里尔克

1903年4月23日，意大利

比萨，维亚雷焦

第四封信

十天前我又苦恼又疲倦地离开了巴黎，到了一处广大的北方的平原，它的旷远、寂静与天空本应使我恢复健康。可是我却走入一个雨的季节，直到今天在风势不定的田野上才闪透出光来；于是我就用这第一瞬间的光明来问候你，亲爱的先生。

亲爱的卡卜斯先生：我很久没有答复你的信，我并没有忘记它——反而它是常常使我从许多信中检出来再读一遍的，并且在你的信里我认识你非常亲切。那是你5月2日的信，你一定记得起这封信。我现在在这远方无边寂静中重读你的信，你那对于生活的美好的忧虑感动我，比我在巴黎时已经感到的还深；在巴黎因为过分

的喧嚣，一切都发出异样的声音，使万物战栗。这里周围是伟大的田野，从海上吹来阵阵的风，这里我觉得，那些问题与情感在它们的深处自有它们本来的生命，没有人能够给你解答；因为就是最好的字句也要失去真意，如果它们要解释那最轻妙、几乎不可言说的事物。虽然，我却相信你不会永远得不到解决，若是你委身于那同现在使我的眼目为之一新的相类似的事物。若是你依托自然，依托自然中的单纯，依托于那几乎没人注意到的渺小，这渺小会不知不觉地变得庞大而不能测度；若是你对于微小都怀有这样的爱，作为一个侍奉者质朴地去赢得一些好像贫穷的事物的信赖，那么，一切对于你就较为轻易、较为一致、较为容易和解了，也许不是在那惊讶着退却的理智中，而是在你最深的意识、觉醒与悟解中得到和解。你是这样年轻，一切都在开始，亲爱的先生，我要尽我的所能请求你，对于你心里一切的疑难要多多忍耐，要去爱这些“问题的本身”，像是爱一间锁闭了的房屋，或是一本用别种文字写成的书。现在你不要去追求那些你还不能得到的答案，因为你还不能在生活里体验到它们。一切都要亲身生活。现在你就在这些问题里“生活”吧。或者，不大注意，渐渐会有那遥远的

一天，你生活到了能解答这些问题的境地。也许你自身内就负有可能性：去组织、去形成一种特别幸福与纯洁的生活方式；你要向那方面修养——但是，无论什么来到，你都要以广大的信任领受；如果它是从你的意志里、从任何一种内身的窘困里产生的，那么你要好好地负担着它，什么也不要憎恶——“性”，是很难的。可是我们分内的事都很难；其实一切严肃的事都是艰难的，而一切又是严肃的。如果你认识了这一层，并且肯这样从你自身，从你的禀性，从你的经验、你的童年、你的生命力出发，得到一种完全自己的（不是被因袭和习俗所影响的）对于“性”的关系，那么你就不要怕你有所迷惑，或是玷污了你最好的所有。

身体的快感是一种感官的体验，与净洁的观赏或是一个甜美的果实放在我们舌上的净洁的感觉没有什么不同；它是我们所应得的丰富而无穷的经验，是一种对于世界的领悟，是一切领悟的丰富与光华。我们感受身体的快感并不是坏事。所不好的是：几乎一切人都错用了、浪费了这种经验，把它放在生命疲倦的地方当作刺激，当作疏散，而不当作向着顶点的聚精会神。就是饮食，也有许多人使之失去了本意：一方面是“不足”，另一方

面是“过度”，都搅混了这个需要的明朗；同样搅混的，是那些生命借以自新的一切深的、单纯的需要。但是一个“个人”能够把它认清，很清晰地生活（如果因为“个人”是要有条件的，那么我们就说是“寂寞的人”），他能够想起，动物和植物中一切的美就是一种爱与渴望的、静静延续着的形式；他能够同看植物一样去看动物，它们忍耐而驯顺地结合、增殖、生长，不是由于生理的享乐也不是由于生理的痛苦，只是顺从需要，这个需要是要比享乐与痛苦伟大，比意志与抵抗还有力。啊，人们要更谦虚地去接受、更严肃地负担这充满大地一直到极小的物体的神秘，并且去承受和感觉，它是怎样重大的艰难，不要把它看得过于容易！对于那只有“一个”的果实，不管它是身体的或是精神的，要有敬畏的心；因为精神的创造也是源于生理的创造，同属于一个本质，并且只像是一种身体快感的更轻妙、更兴奋、更有永久性的再现。至于你所说的“那个思想，去当创造者，去生产、去制作”，绝不能缺少他在世界中得到不断的伟大的证明和实现，也不能缺少从物与动物那里得来的千应万诺——他的享受也只是因此才这样难以形容地美丽而丰富，因为他具有从数百万制作与生产中遗传下来的回

忆。在一个创造者思想里会有千百个被人忘记的爱情的良宵又重新苏醒，它们以崇高的情绪填实这个思想。并且那夜间幽会、结合在狂欢中的爱人们，是在做一种严肃的工作，聚集起无数的温存，为任何一个将来后起的诗人的诗歌预备下深厚的力量，去说那难于言说的欢乐。他们把“将来”唤来；纵使他们迷惑，盲目地拥抱，“将来”终于是要到的，一个新人在生长，这里完成一个偶然，在偶然的根处有永恒的规律醒来，一颗富于抵抗的种子就以这个规律闯入那对面迎来的卵球。你不要为表面所误；在深处一切都成为规律。那些把这种神秘虚伪而错误地去生活的人（这样的人本来很多），只是自己失掉了它，而把它往下传递，像是密封的信件，并不知它的内容。你也不要被名称的繁多和事物的复杂所迷惑。超越一切的也许是一个伟大的“母性”作为共同的渴望。那少女的、一种“还无所作为”（你这样说的很好）的本性的美是，它预感着、准备着，悚惧着、渴望着的母性。母亲的美是正在尽职的母性；一个丰富的回忆则存在于老妇的身内。但我以为在男人身内也有母性，无论是身体的或是精神的；他的创造也是一种生产，只要是从最内在的丰满中创造出来的便是生产。大半两性间的关系

比人们平素所想的更密切，也许这世界伟大的革新就在于这一点：男人同女人从一切错误的感觉与嫌忌里解放出来，不作为对立面互相寻找，而彼此是兄妹或邻居一般，共同以“人”的立场去工作，以便简捷地、严肃而忍耐地负担那放在他们肩上的艰难的“性”。

凡是将来有一天许多人或能实现的事，现在寂寞的人已经可以起始准备了，用他比较确切的双手来建造。亲爱的先生，所以你要爱你的寂寞，负担那它以悠扬的怨诉给你引来的痛苦。你说，你身边的都同你疏远了，其实这就是你周围扩大的开始。如果你的亲近都离远了，那么你的旷远已经在星空下开展得很广大；你要为你的成长欢喜，可是向那里你不能带进来一个人，要好好对待那些落在后边的人，在他们面前你要稳定自若，不要用你的怀疑苦恼他们，也不要用你的信心或欢悦惊吓他们，这是他们所不能了解的。同他们寻找出一种简单而诚挚的谐和，这种谐和，任凭你自己将来怎么转变，都无须更改；要爱惜他们那种生疏方式的生活，要谅解那些进入老境的人；他们对于你所信任的孤独是畏惧的。要避免去给那在父母与子女间常演出的戏剧增加材料；这要费去许多子女的力，消蚀许多父母的爱，纵使他们

的爱不了解我们；究竟是在爱着、温暖着我们。不要向他们问计，也不要计较了解；但要相信那种为你保存下来像是一份遗产似的爱，你要信任在这爱中自有力量存在，自有一种幸福，无须脱离这个幸福才能扩大你的世界。

那很好，你先进入一个职业[1]，它使你成为独立的人，事事完全由你自己料理。你耐心地等着吧，看你内心的生活是不是由于这职业的形式而受到限制。我认为这职业是很艰难很不容易对付的，因为它被广大的习俗所累，并且不容人对于它的问题有个人的意见存在。但是你的寂寞将在这些很生疏的关系中间是你的立足点和家乡，从这里出来你将寻得你一切的道路。

我一切的祝愿都在陪伴着你，我信任你。

你的：赖内·马利亚·里尔克

1903 年 7 月 16 日，不来梅（Bremen）

沃普斯韦德（Worpswede）

1. 卡卜斯被任命为奥地利军官。

第五封信

亲爱的、尊敬的先生:

我在佛罗伦萨收到你 8 月 29 日的信，现在——两个月了——我才写回信告诉你。请你原谅我的迟延——我在路上不喜欢写信，因为我写信除去必需的纸笔外还要用: 一些幽静、寂寞和一个不太生疏的时刻。

我们在六个星期前到了罗马，那时还是个空虚、炎热、时疫流行的罗马，这种环境又添上许多现实生活上安排的困难，更助长围绕我们的不安，简直没有终结，使我们尝尽了异乡漂泊的痛苦。更加之以: 罗马（如果我们还不认识它）在我们到达的头几天真令人窒闷悲哀——由于它放射出来的死气沉沉忧郁的博物馆的空气;

由于它精华已尽，而又勉强保持着的过去时代的储存（从中滋养着一个可怜的现在）；由于这些，无名的、被学者和语言学家们所维护、经常不断的意大利旅游者所效仿的、对于一切改头换面或是毁败了的物品的过分的估价，根本这些物品也不过是另一个时代另一种生活的偶然的残余，这生活已经不是我们的了，而也不应该是我们的。在日日担心防范的几个星期后，虽还有些纷乱，却终于回到自己的世界，我们才说：这里并不比别的地方有更多的美，这些被世世代代所叹赏的对象，都经过俗手的修补，没有意义，无所包含，没有精神，没有价值——但这里也自有许多美，因为无论什么地方都有它的美。永远生动的流水从古老的沟渠流入这座大城，它们在许多广场的白石盘上欢舞，散入宽阔的贮水池中，昼间泠泠有声，夜晚的声音更为清澈，这里的夜色广大而星光灿烂，拂着习习轻风。并且有许多名园，使人难忘的林荫路与石阶——米霞盎基罗[1]所设计的石阶，那是按着向下流水的姿势建筑的石阶：宽宽地向下一层生出一层，像是后浪接着前浪。由于这样的印象，我们凝聚精

1. 米霞盎基罗（Michelangelo，1475—1564），意大利文艺复兴时期的雕刻家、画家兼诗人。

神，从那些傲慢的、谈谈讲讲的“多数”（那是多么爱饶舌呀！）回到自身内，慢慢地学习认识“少数”，在少数的事物里延绵着我们所爱的永恒和我们轻轻地分担着的寂寞。

现在我还住在城内卡皮托丘上[1]，离那最美的从罗马艺术中保存下来的马克·奥雷尔[2]骑马式的石像不远；但是在几个星期后我将迁入一个寂静而简单的地方，是一座老的望楼，它深深地消失在一片大园林里，足以躲避城市的喧嚣与纷扰。我将要在那里住一冬，享受那无边的寂静，从这寂静中我期待着良好而丰盛的时间的赠品……

到那时我将常常在家，再给你写较长的信，还要谈到关于你信中的事。今天我必须告诉你的是（这已经是不对了，我没有早一点告诉你），你信中提到的那本书（其中想必有你的作品）没有寄到。是不是从沃普斯韦德给你退回去了（因为包裹不能转到外国）？退回是最好的，我愿意得到证实。希望不要遗失——这在意大利

---

1. 卡皮托（Kapitoe），罗马七座山丘中的一座。

2. 马克·奥雷尔（Marc Aurel，118—180），罗马皇帝，著有《随感录》流传后世。

的邮务并不是例外的事——可惜。

我很愿意接到这本书（像是我愿意接到你所写的一切一样）；还有你最近的诗（如果你寄给我），我要永远尽我的所能诚心地一读再读，好好体验。

以多多的愿望和祝福：

你的赖内 · 马利亚 · 里尔克

1903 年 10 月 29 日，罗马

第六封信

我的亲爱的卡卜斯先生:

你不会得不到我的祝愿，如果圣诞节到了，你在这节日中比往日更深沉地负担着你的寂寞。若是你觉得它过于广大，那么你要因此而欢喜（你问你自己吧），哪有寂寞，不是广大的呢；我们只有“一个”寂寞又大又不容易负担，并且几乎人人都有这危险的时刻，他们情心愿意把寂寞和任何一种庸俗无聊的社交，和与任何一个不相配的人勉强谐和的假象去交换……但也许正是这些时候，寂寞在生长；它的生长是痛苦的，像是男孩的发育，是悲哀的，像是春的开始。你不要为此而迷惑。我们最需要的却只是：寂寞，广大的内心的寂寞。“走向内

心”，长时期不遇一人——这我们必须能够做到。居于寂寞，像人们在儿童时那样寂寞，成人们来来往往，跟一些好像很重要的事务纠缠，大人们是那样匆忙，可是儿童并不懂得他们做些什么事。

如果一天我们洞察到他们的事务是贫乏的，他们的职业是枯僵的，跟生命没有关联，那么我们为什么不从自己世界的深处，从自己寂寞的广处（这寂寞的本身就是工作、地位、职业），和儿童一样把它们当作一种生疏的事去观看呢？为什么把一个儿童聪明的“不解”抛开，而对于许多事物采取防御和蔑视的态度呢？“不解”是居于寂寞；防御与蔑视虽说是要设法和这些事物隔离，同时却是和它们发生纠葛了。

亲爱的先生，你去思考你自身负担着的世界；至于怎样称呼这思考，那就随你的心意了；不管是自己童年的回忆，或是对于自己将来的想望——只是要多多注意从你生命里出现的事物，要把它放在你周围所看到的一切之上。你最内心的事物值得你全心全意地去爱，你必须为它多方工作；并且不要浪费许多时间和精力去解释你对于人们的态度。“到底谁向你说，你本来有一个态度呢？——我知道你的职业是枯燥的，处处和你相违背，

我早已看出你的苦恼，我知道，它将要来了。现在它来了，我不能排解你的苦恼，我只能劝你去想一想，是不是一切职业都是这样，向个人尽是无理的要求，尽是敌意，它同样也饱受了许多低声忍气、不满于那枯燥的职责的人们的憎恶。你要知道，你现在必须应付的职业并不见得比旁的职业被什么习俗呀、偏见呀、谬误呀连累得更厉害；若是真有些炫耀着一种更大的自由的职业，那就不会有职业在它自身内广远而宽阔，和那些从中组成真实生活的伟大事物相通了。只有寂寞的个人，他跟一个“物”一样被放置在深邃的自然规律下，当他走向刚破晓的早晨，或是向外望那充满非常事件的夜晚，当他感觉到那里发生什么事，一切地位便会脱离了他，像是脱离一个死者，纵使他正处在真正的生活的中途。亲爱的卡卜斯先生，凡是你现在做军官所必须经验的，你也许在任何一种现有的职业里都会感到，甚至纵使你脱离各种职务，独自同社会寻找一种轻易而独立的接触，这种压迫之感也不会对你有什么减轻——到处都是一样，但是这并不足使我们恐惧悲哀；如果你在人我之间没有谐和，你就试行与物接近，它们不会遗弃你；还有夜，还有风——那吹过树林、掠过田野的风；在物中间

和动物那里，一切都充满了你可以分担的事；还有儿童，他们同你在儿时所经验过的一样，又悲哀，又幸福——如果你想起你的童年，你就又在那些寂寞的儿童中间了，成人们是无所谓的，他们的尊严没有价值。

若是你因为对于童年时到处可以出现的神已经不能信仰，想到童年，想到与它相连的那种单纯和寂静，而感到苦恼不安，那么，亲爱的卡卜斯先生，你问一问自己，你是不是真把神失落了？也许正相反，你从来没有得到他？什么时候应该有过神呢？你相信吗，关于神，一个儿童能够把住他，成人们只能费力去负担他，而他的重量足以把老人压倒？你相信吗，谁当真有他，又能把他像一块小石片似的失落？或者你也不以为吗，谁有过他，还只能被他丢掉？——但如果你认识到，他在你的童年不曾有过，从前也没有生存过；如果你觉得基督是被他的渴望所欺，穆罕默德是被他的骄傲所骗——如果你惊愕地感到，就是现在，就是我们谈他的这个时刻，他也没有存在——那么，什么给你以权利，觉得缺少这从来不曾有过的神像是丧失一个亡人，并且寻找他像是找一件遗失的物品呢？

你为什么不这样想，想他是将要来到的，他要从永

恒里降生，是一棵树上最后的果实，我们不过是这树上的树叶？是谁阻拦你，不让你把他的诞生放在将来转变的时代，不让你度过你的一生像是度过这伟大的孕期内又痛苦又美丽的一日？你没有看见吗，一切发生的事怎样总是重新开始？那就不能是神的开始吗？啊，开端的本身永远是这般美丽！如果他是最完全的，那么较为微小的事物在他以前就不应该存在吗，以便他从丰满与过剩中能够有所选择？——他不应该是个最后者吗，将一切握诸怀抱？若是我们所希求的他早已过去了，那我们还有什么意义呢？

像是蜜蜂酿蜜那样，我们从万物中采撷最甜美的资料来建造我们的神。我们甚至以渺小，没有光彩的事物开始（只要是由于爱），我们以工作，继之以休息，以一种沉默，或是以一种微小的寂寞的欢悦，以我们没有朋友、没有同伴单独所做的一切来建造他，他，我们并不能看到，正如我们的祖先不能看见我们一样。可是那些久已逝去的人，依然存在于我们的生命里，作为我们的禀赋，作为我们命运的负担，作为循环着的血液，作为从时间的深处升发出来的姿态。

现在你所希望不到的事，将来不会有一天在最遥远、

最终极的神的那里实现吗?

亲爱的卡卜斯先生，在这虔诚的情感中庆祝你的圣诞节吧，也许神正要用你这生命的恐惧来开始；你过的这几天也许正是一切在你生命里为他工作的时期，正如你在儿时已经有一次很辛苦地为他工作过一样。好好地忍耐，不要沮丧，你想，如果春天要来，大地就使它一点点地完成，我们所能做的最少量的工作，不会使神的生成比起大地之于春天更为艰难。

祝你快乐，勇敢!

你的：赖内·马利亚·里尔克

1903 年 12 月 23 日，罗马

第七封信

我的亲爱的卡卜斯先生:

自从我接到你上次的来信，已经过了许久。请你不要见怪。先是工作，随后是事务的干扰，最后是小病，总阻挡着我给你写回信，因为我给你写信是要在良好平静的时刻。现在我觉得好些了（初春的恶劣多变的过渡时期在这里也使人觉得很不舒适），亲爱的卡卜斯先生，我问候你，并且（这是我衷心愿做的事）就我所知道的来回答你。

你看，我把你的十四行诗抄下来了，因为我觉得它美丽简练，是在很适当的形式里产生的。在我所读到的你的诗中，这是最好的一首。现在我又把它誊抄给你，

因为我以为这很有意义，并且充满新鲜的体验，在别人的笔下又看到自己的作品。你读这首诗，像是别人作的，可是你将要在最深处感到它怎样更是你的。

这是我的一种快乐，常常读这首十四行诗和你的来信；为了这两件事我感谢你。

在寂寞中你不要彷徨迷惑，由于你自身内有一些愿望要从这寂寞里脱身——也正是这个愿望，如果你平静地、卓越地，像一件工具似的去运用它，它就会帮助你把你的寂寞扩展到广远的地方。一般人（用因袭的帮助）把一切都轻易地去解决，而且按着轻易中最轻易的方面；但这是很显然的，我们必须认定艰难；凡是生存者都认定，自然界中一切都是按照自己的方式生长，防御，表现出来自己，无论如何都要生存，抵抗一切反对的力量。我们知道的很少；但我们必须委身于艰难却是一件永不会丢开我们的信念。寂寞地生存是好的，因为寂寞是艰难的；只要是艰难的事，就有使我们更有理由为它工作。

爱，很好，因为爱是艰难的。以人去爱人：这也许是给与我们的最艰难、最重大的事，是最后的实验与考试，是最高的工作，别的工作都不过是为此而做的准备。所以一切正在开始的青年们还不能爱；他们必须学

习。他们必须用他们整个的生命、用一切的力量，集聚他们寂寞、痛苦和向上激动的心去学习爱。可是学习的时期永远是一个长久的专心致志的时期，爱就长期地深深地侵入生命——寂寞，增强而深入的孤独生活，是为了爱着的人。爱的要义并不是什么倾心、献身、与第二者结合（那该是怎样的一个结合呢，如果是一种不明了，无所成就、不关重要的结合？），它对于个人是一种崇高的动力，去成熟，在自身内有所完成，去完成一个世界，是为了另一个人完成一个自己的世界，这对于他是一个巨大的、不让步的要求，把他选择出来，向广远召唤。青年们只应在把这当作课业去工作的意义中（“昼夜不停地探索，去锤炼”）去使用那给予他们的爱。至于倾心、献身，以及一切的结合，还不是他们的事（他们还须长时间地节省、聚集），那是最后的终点，也许是人的生活现在还几乎不能达到的境地。

但是青年们在这方面常常错误得这样深（因为在他们本性中没有忍耐），如果爱到了他们身上，他们便把生命任意抛掷，甚至陷入窒闷、颠倒、紊乱的状态——但随后又该怎样呢？这支离破碎的聚合（他们自己叫作结合，还愿意称为幸福），还能使生活有什么成就吗？能过

得去吗？他们的将来呢？这其间每个人都为了别人失掉自己，同时也失掉别人，并且失掉许多还要来到的别人，失掉许多广远与可能性；把那些轻微的充满预感的物体的接近与疏远，改换成一个日暮穷途的景况，什么也不能产生：无非是一些厌恶、失望与贫乏，不得已时便在因袭中寻求补救，有大宗因袭的条例早已准备好了，像是避祸亭一般在这危验的路旁。在各种人类的生活中没有比爱被因袭的习俗附饰得更多的了，是无所不用其极地发明许多救生圈、游泳袋、救护船；社会上的理解用各种样式设备下避难所，因为它倾向于把爱的生活也看作一种娱乐，所以必须轻率地把它形成一种简易、平稳、毫无险阻的生活，跟一切公开的娱乐一样。

诚然也有许多青年错误地去爱，即随随便便地赠予，不能寂寞（一般总是止于这种境地——），他们感到一种失误的压迫，要按照他们自己个人的方式使他们已经陷入的境域变得富有生力和成果——因为他们的天性告诉他们，爱的众多问题还比不上其他的重要的事体，它们可以公开地按照这样或那样的约定来解决；都不过是人与人之间切身问题，它们需要一个在各种情况下都新鲜而特殊、“只是”个人的回答——但，他们已经互相抛掷

在一起，再也不能辨别、区分，再也不据有自己的所有，他们怎么能够从他们自身内从这已经埋没的寂寞的深处寻得一条出路呢？

他们的行为都是在通常无可告援的情势下产生的，如果他们以最好的意愿要躲避那落在他们身上的习俗（譬如说结婚），也还是陷入一种不寻常，但仍同样是死气沉沉限于习俗的解决的网中。因为他们周围的一切都是——习俗：从一种很早就聚在一起的、暗淡的结合中表演出来的只是种种限于习俗的行动；这样的紊乱昏迷之所趋的每个关系，都有它的习俗，即使是那最不常见的（普通的意义叫作不道德的）也在内；是的，甚至于“分离”也几乎是一种习俗的步骤，是一种非个性的偶然的决断，没有力量，没有成果。

谁严肃地看，谁就感到，同对于艰难的“死”一样，对于这艰难的“爱”还没有启蒙，还没有解决，还没有什么指示与道路被认识；并且为了我们蒙蔽着、负担着、传递下去，还没有显现的这两个任务，也没有共同的、协议可靠的规律供我们探讨。但是在我们只作为单独的个人起始练习生活的程度内，这些伟大的事物将同单独的个人们在更接近的亲切中相遇。艰难的爱的工作对于

我们发展过程的要求是无限的广大，我们作为信从者对于那些要求还不能胜任。但是，如果我们坚持忍耐，把爱作为重担和学业担在肩上，而不在任何浅易和轻浮的游戏中失掉自己（许多人都是一到他们生存中最严肃的严肃面前，便隐藏在游戏的身后）——那么将来继我们而来的人们或许会感到一点小小的进步与减轻；这就够好了。

可是我们现在正应该对于一个单独的人和另一个单独的人的关系，没有成见、如实地观察，我们试验看在这种关系里生活，面前并没有前例。可是在时代的变更中已经有些事，对于我们小心翼翼的开端能有所帮助了。

少女和妇女，在她们新近自己的发展中，只暂时成为男人恶习与特性的模仿者，男人职业的重演者。经过这样不稳定的过程后，事实会告诉我们，妇女只是从那（常常很可笑的）乔装的成功与变化中走过，以便把她们自己的天性从男性歪曲的影响中洗净。至于真的生命是更直接、更丰富、更亲切地在妇女的身内，根本上她们早应该变成比男人更纯净、更人性的人；男人没有身体的果实，只生活于生活的表面之下，傲慢而急躁，看

轻他们要去爱的事物。如果妇女将来把这“只是女性”的习俗在她们外生活的转变中脱去，随后那从痛苦与压迫里产生出的妇女的“人性”就要见诸天日了，这是男人们现在还没有感到的，到那时他们将从中受到惊奇和打击。有一天（现在北欧的国家里已经有确切的证明）新的少女来到，并且所谓妇女这个名词，她不只是当作男人的对立体来讲，却含有一些独立的意义，使我们不再想到“补充”与“界限”，只想到生命与生存——女性的人。

这个进步将要把现在谬误的爱的生活转变（违背着落伍的男人们的意志），从根本更改，形成一种人对于人，不是男人对于女人的关系。并且这更人性的爱（它无限地谨慎而精细，良好而明晰地在结合与解脱中完成），它将要同我们辛辛苦苦地预备着的爱相似，它存在于这样的情况里：两个寂寞相爱护，相区分，相敬重。

还有：你不要以为，那在你童年曾经有过一次的伟大的爱已经失却了；你能说吗，那时并没有伟大的良好的愿望在你的生命里成熟，而且现在你还从中吸取养分？我相信那个爱是强有力地永在你的回忆中，因为它是你第一次的深的寂寞，也是你为你生命所做的第一次

的内心的工作——祝你一切安好，亲爱的卡卜斯先生！

你的：赖内·马利亚·里尔克

1904 年 5 月 14 日，罗马

十四行诗

我生命里有一缕阴深的苦恼
颤动，它不叹息，也不抱怨。
我梦里边雪一般的花片
是我寂静的长日的祭祷。

但是大问题梗住我的小道。
我变得渺小而凄凉
像是走过一座湖旁，
我不敢量一量湖水的波涛。

一种悲哀侵袭我，这般愁惨
好似暗淡的夏夜的苍茫

时时闪露出一点星光；

于是我的双手向着爱试探，
因为我想祈求那样的声调，
我热烈的口边还不能找到……

（弗兰斯·卡卜斯）

第八封信

亲爱的卡卜斯先生，我想再和你谈一谈，虽然我几乎不能说对你有所帮助以及对你有一些用处的话。你有过很多大的悲哀，这些悲哀都已过去了。你说，这悲哀的过去也使你非常苦恼。但是，请你想一想，是不是这些大的悲哀并不曾由你生命的中心走过？当你悲哀的时候，是不是在你生命里并没有许多变化，在你本性的任何地方也无所改变？危险而恶劣的是那些悲哀，我们把它们运送到人群中，以遮盖它们的声音；像是敷敷衍衍治疗的病症，只是暂时退却，过些时又更可怕地发作；它们聚集在体内，成为一种没有生活过、被摈斥、被遗弃的生命，能使我们死去。如果我

们能比我们平素的知识所能达到的地方看得更远一点，稍微越过我们预感的前哨，那么也许我们将会以比担当我们的欢悦更大的信赖去担当我们的悲哀。因为它们（悲哀）都是那些时刻，正当一些新的、陌生的事物侵入我们的生命；我们的情感蜷伏于怯懦的局促的状态里，一切都退却，形成一种寂静，于是这无人认识的“新”就立在中间，沉默无语。

我相信几乎我们一切的悲哀都是紧张的瞬间，这时我们感到麻木，因为我们不再听到诧异的情感生存。因为我们要同这生疏的闯入者独自周旋；因为我们平素所信任的与习惯的都暂时离开了我们；因为我们正处在一个不能容我们立足的过程中。可是一旦这不期而至的新事物迈进我们的生命，走进我们的心房，在心的最深处化为无有，溶解在我们的血液中，悲哀也就因此过去了。我们再也经验不到当时的情形。这很容易使我们相信前此并没有什么发生；其实我们却是改变了，正如一所房子，走进一位新客，它改变了。我们不能说，是谁来了，我们往后也许不知道，可是有许多迹象告诉我们，在“未来”还没有发生之前，它就以这样的方式潜入我们的生命，以便在我们身内变化。所以我们在悲哀

的时刻要安于寂寞，多注意，这是很重要的，因为当我们的“未来”潜入我们的生命的瞬间，好像是空虚而枯僵，但与那从外边来的、为我们发生的喧嚣而意外的时刻相比，是同生命接近得多。我们悲哀时越沉静，越忍耐，越坦白，这新的事物也越深、越清晰地走进我们的生命，我们也就更好地保护它，它也就更多地成为我们自己的命运；将来有一天它“发生”了（就是说：它从我们的生命里出来向着别人走进），我们将在最内心的地方感到我们同它亲切而接近。并且这是必要的。是必要的——我们将渐渐地向那方面发展——凡是迎面而来的事，是没有生疏的，都早已属于我们了。人们已经变换过这么多运转的定义，将来会渐渐认清，我们所谓的命运是从我们“人”里出来，并不是从外边向着我们“人”走进。只因为有许多人，当命运在他们身内生存时，他们不曾把它吸收，化为己有，所以他们也认不清，有什么从他们身内出现；甚至如此生疏，他们在仓皇恐惧之际，以为命运一定是正在这时走进他们的生命，因为他们确信自己从来没有见过这样类似的事物。正如对于太阳的运转曾经有过长期的蒙惑那样，现在人们对于未来的运转，也还在同样地自欺自蔽。其实“未

来”站得很稳，亲爱的卡卜斯先生，但是我们动转在这无穷无尽的空间。

我们怎么能不感觉困难呢？

如果我们再谈到寂寞，那就会更明显，它根本不是我们所能选择或弃舍的事物。我们都是寂寞的。人能够自欺，好像并不寂寞。只不过如此而已。但是，那有多么好呢，如果我们一旦看出，我们都正在脱开这欺骗的局面。在其间我们自然要发生眩昏；因为平素我们的眼睛看惯了的一切这时都忽然失去，再也没有亲近的事物，一切的远方都是无穷的旷远。谁从他的屋内没有准备，没有过程，忽然被移置在一脉高山的顶上，他必会有类似的感觉；一种无与伦比的不安被交付给无名的事物，几乎要把他毁灭。他或许想象会跌落，或者相信会被抛掷在天空，或者粉身碎骨，他的头脑必须发现多么大的谎话，去补救、去说明他官感迷失的状态。一切的距离与尺度对于那寂寞的人就有了变化；从这些变化中忽然会有许多变化发生。跟在山顶上的那个人一样，生出许多非常的想象与稀奇的感觉，它们好像超越了一切能够担当的事体。但那是必要的，我们也体验这种情况。我们必须尽量广阔地承受我们的生存；一切，甚至

闻所未闻的事物，都可能在里边存在。根本那是我们被要求的唯一的勇气：勇敢地面向我们所能遇到的最稀奇、最吃惊、最不可解的事物。就因为许多人在这意义中是怯懦的，所以使生活受了无限的损伤；人们称作“奇象”的那些体验、所谓“幽灵世界”、死，以及一切同我们相关联的事物，它们都被我们日常的防御挤出生活之外，甚至我们能够接受它们的感官都枯萎了。关于“神”，简直就不能谈论了。但是对于不可解的事物的恐惧，不仅使个人的生存更为贫乏，并且人与人的关系也因之受到限制，正如从有无限可能性的河床里捞出来，放在一块荒芜不毛的岸上。因为这不仅是一种惰性，使人间的关系极为单调而陈腐地把旧事一再重演，而且是对于任何一种不能预测、不堪胜任的新的生活的畏缩。但是如果有人对于一切有了准备，无论什么，甚至最大的哑谜，也不置之度外，那么他就会把同别人的关系，当作生动着的事物去体验，甚至充分理解自己的存在。正如我们把各个人的存在看成一块较大或较小的空间，那么大部分人却只认识了他们空间的一角、一块窗前的空地，或是他们走来走去的一条窄道。这样他们就有一定的安定。可是那危险的不安定是更人性的，它

能促使爱伦 · 坡[1]的故事里的囚犯摸索他们可怕的牢狱的形状，而熟悉他们住处内不可言喻的恐怖。但我们不是囚犯，没有人在我们周围布置了陷阱，没有什么来恐吓我们，苦恼我们。我们在生活中像是在最适合于我们的原素里，况且我们经过几千年之久的适应和生活这样地相似了，如果我们静止不动，凭借一种成功的模拟，便很难同我们周围的一切有所区分。我们没有理由不信任我们的世界，因为它并不敌对我们。如果它有恐惧，就是我们的恐惧；它有难测的深渊，这深渊是属于我们的；有危险，我们就必须试行去爱这些危险。若是我们把我们的生活，按照那叫我们必须永远把握艰难的原则来处理，那么现在还最生疏的事物就会变得最亲切、最忠实的了。我们怎么能忘却那各民族原始时都有过的神话呢；恶龙在最紧急的瞬间变成公主的那段神话；也许我们生活中一切的恶龙都是公主们，她们只是等候着，美丽而勇敢地看一看我们。也许一切恐怖的事物在最深处是无

1. 爱伦 · 坡（Allan Poe，1809—1849），美国小说家、诗人，以描写神秘恐怖故事知名。这里指的是他的一篇小说《深坑和钟摆》（*The Pit and the Pendulum*），描述一个被判处死刑的人在黑暗的牢狱里摸索墙壁、猜度牢狱形状的恐怖情况。

助的，向我们要求救助。

亲爱的卡卜斯先生，如果有一种悲哀在你面前出现，它是从未见过的那样广大，如果有一种不安，像光与云影似的掠过你的行为与一切工作，你不要恐惧。你必须想，那是有些事在你身边发生了；那是生活没有忘记你，它把你握在手中，它永不会让你失落。为什么你要把一种不安、一种痛苦、一种忧郁置于你的生活之外呢，可是你还不知道，这些情况在为你做什么工作。为什么你要这样追问，这一切是从哪里来，要向哪里去呢？可是你要知道，你是在过渡中，要愿望自己有所变化。如果你的过程里有一些是病态的，你要想一想，病就是一种方法，有机体用以从生疏的事物中解放出来；所以我们只需让它生病，使它有整个的病发作，因为这才是进步。亲爱的卡卜斯先生，现在你自身内有这么多的事发生，你要像一个病人似的忍耐，又像一个康复者似的自信；你也许同时是这两个人。并且你还须是看护自己的医生。但是在病中常常有许多天，医生除了等候以外，什么事也不能做。这就是（尽你是你的医生的时候），现在首先必须做的事。

对于自己不要过甚地观察。不要从对你发生的事物

中求得很快的结论，让它们单纯地自生自长吧。不然你就很容易用种种（所谓道德的）谴责回顾你的过去，这些过去自然和你现在遇到的一切很有关系。凡是从你童年的迷途、愿望、渴望中在你身内继续影响着的事，它们并不让你回忆，供你评判。一个寂寞而孤单的童年非常的情况是这样艰难，这样复杂，受到这么多外来的影响，同时又这样脱开了一切现实生活的关联，纵使在童年有罪恶，我们也不该简捷了当地称作罪恶。对于许多名称，必须多多注意；常常只是犯罪的名称使生命为之破碎，而不是那无名的、个人的行为本身，至于这个行为也许是生活中规定的必要，能被生活轻易接受的。因为你把胜利估量得过高，所以你觉得力的消耗如此巨大；胜利并不是你认为已经完成的“伟大”，纵使你觉得正确；“伟大”是你能以一些真的、实在的事物代替欺骗。不然你的胜利也不过是一种道德上的反应，没有广大的意义，但是它却成为你生活的一个段落。亲爱的卡卜斯先生，关于你的生活，我有很多的愿望。你还记得吗，这个生活是怎样从童年里出来，向着“伟大”渴望？我看着，它现在又从这些伟大前进，渴望更伟大的事物。所以艰难的生活永无止境，但因此生长也无止境。

如果我还应该向你说一件事，那么就是：你不要相信，那试行劝慰你的人是无忧无虑地生活在那些有时对你有益的简单而平静的几句话里。他的生活有许多的辛苦与悲哀，他远远地专诚帮助你。不然，他就绝不能找到那几句话。

你的：赖内·马利亚·里尔克

1904 年 8 月 12 日，瑞典

弗拉底（Flädie），滤格比庄园（Borgeby Càrb）

第九封信

我亲爱的卡卜斯先生:

在这没有通信的时期内，我一半是在旅途上，一半是事务匆忙，使我不能写信。今天我写信也是困难的，因为我已经写了许多封，手都疲倦了。若是我能以口述给旁人写，我还能向你说许多，可是现在你只好接受这寥寥几行来报答你的长信。

亲爱的卡卜斯先生，我常常思念你，并且以这样专诚的愿望思念你，总要对你有所帮助。但是我的信到底能不能帮助你，我却常常怀疑。你不要说：它们能够帮助你。你只安心接受这些信吧，不必说感谢的话，让我们等着，看将要有什么事情来到。

现在我对于你信里个别的字句加以探讨，大半是没有用的；因为我关于你疑惑的倾向，关于体内外生活和谐的不可能，关于另外苦恼着你的一切——我所能说的，还依然是我已经说过的话：还是愿你自己有充分的忍耐去担当，有充分单纯的心去信仰；你将会越来越信任艰难的事物和你在众人中间感到的寂寞。以外就是让生活自然进展。请你相信：无论如何，生活是合理的。

谈到情感：凡是使你集中向上的情感都是纯洁的，但那只捉住你本性的一方面，对你有所伤害的情感是不纯洁的。凡是在你童年能想到的事都是好的。凡能够使你比你从前最美好的时刻还更丰富的，都是对的。各种提高都是好的，如果它是在你“全”血液中，如果它不是迷醉，不是忧郁，而是透明到底的欢悦。你了解我的意思吗？

就是你的怀疑也可以成为一种好的特性，若是你好好“培养”它。它必须成为明智的，它必须成为批判——当它要伤害你一些事物时，你要问它，这些事物“为什么”丑恶，向它要求证据，考问它，你也许见它仓皇失措，也许见它表示异议。但你不要让步，你同它辩论，每一回都要多多注意，立定脚步，终于有一天它会从一

个破坏者变成你的一个最好的工作者——或许在一切从事于建设你的生活的工作者中它是最聪明的一个。

亲爱的卡卜斯先生，这是我今天所能向你说的一切。我附寄给你我一篇短的作品的抽印本[1]，这是在布拉格出版的《德意志工作》中发表的。在那里我继续着同你谈生和死，以及它们的伟大与美丽。

你的：赖内·马利亚·里尔克

1904 年 11 月 4 日，瑞典

永瑟勒德（Jonsered），弗卢堡（Fruburg）

---

1. 系里尔克的散文诗《旗手克里斯多夫·里尔克的爱与死之歌》（*Die Weise Von Liebe und Tod des Cornets Christoph Rilke*）。

第十封信

亲爱的卡卜斯先生，你该知道，我得你这封美好的信，我是多么欢喜。你给我的消息是真实、诚挚，又像你从前那样，我觉得很好，我越想越感到那实在是好的消息。我本来想在圣诞节的晚间给你写信，但是这一冬我多方从事没有间断的工作，这古老的节日是这样快地走来了，使我没有时间去做我必须处理的事，更少写信。

但是在节日里我常常思念你，我设想你是怎样寂静地在你寂寞的军垒中生活，两旁是空旷的高山，大风从南方袭来，好像要把这些山整块地吞了下去。

这种寂静必须是广大无边，好容许这样的风声风势得以驰骋，如果我想到，更加上那辽远的海也在你面前

同时共奏，像是太古的谐音中最深处的旋律，那么我就希望你能忠实地、忍耐地让这大规模的寂寞在你身上工作，它不再能从你的生命中消灭；在一切你要去生活要去从事的事物中，它永远赓续着像是一种无名的势力，并且将确切地影响你，有如祖先的血在我们身内不断地流动，和我们自己的血混为唯一的、绝无仅有的一体，在我们生命的无论哪一个转折。

是的：我很欢喜，你据有这个固定的、可以言传的存在，有职称，有制服，有任务，有一切把得定、范围得住的事物，它们在这同样孤立而人数不多的军队环境中，接受严肃与必要的工作，它们超越军队职业的游戏与消遣意味着一种警醒的运用，它们不仅容许，而且正好培养自主的注意力。我们要在那些为我们工作、时时置我们于伟大而自然的事物面前的情况中生活，这是必要的一切。

艺术也是一种生活方式，无论我们怎样生活，都能不知不觉地为它准备；每个真实的生活都比那些虚假的、以艺术为号召的职业跟艺术更为接近，它们炫耀一种近似的艺术，实际上却否定了、损伤了艺术的存在，如整个的报章文字、几乎一切的批评界、四分之三号称文学

和要号称文学的作品，都是这样。我很高兴，简捷地说，是因为你经受了易于陷入的危险，寂寞而勇敢地生活在任何一处无情的现实中。即将来到的一年会使你在这样的生活里更为坚定。

你的：赖内·马利亚·里尔克

1908 年，圣诞节第二日，巴黎

PENGUIN

LITTLE BLACK

CLASSICS